DEDICATION

This Tales from Gremela installment is dedicated to the coolest kid I know, Octavia.

TABLE OF CONTENTS

ONE
THE CORONATION - 2

TWO
GALHEIM -14

THREE
THE JOURNEY AHEAD- 25

FOUR
A TALE OF TWO BROTHERS - 35

FIVE
ABOARD THE MARE DOMITOR - 52

SIX
THE CAVE - 63

SEVEN
THE FOREST -73

EIGHT
THE RAGING SEAS - 89

NINE
CENTAURIA - 101

TEN
THE FOREST ONCE MORE – 14

ELEVEN
CENTAURIA AGAIN – 129

TWELVE
THE EVIL WITHIN – 140

THIRTEEN
THE REUNION – 149

FOURTEEN
THE COUNCIL – 158

FIFTEEN
THE ALTAR – 169

SIXTEEN
THE MAGIDEUS – 180

SEVENTEEN
THE MAGIC RETURNS – 191

EIGHTEEN
WHAT COMES NEXT – 200

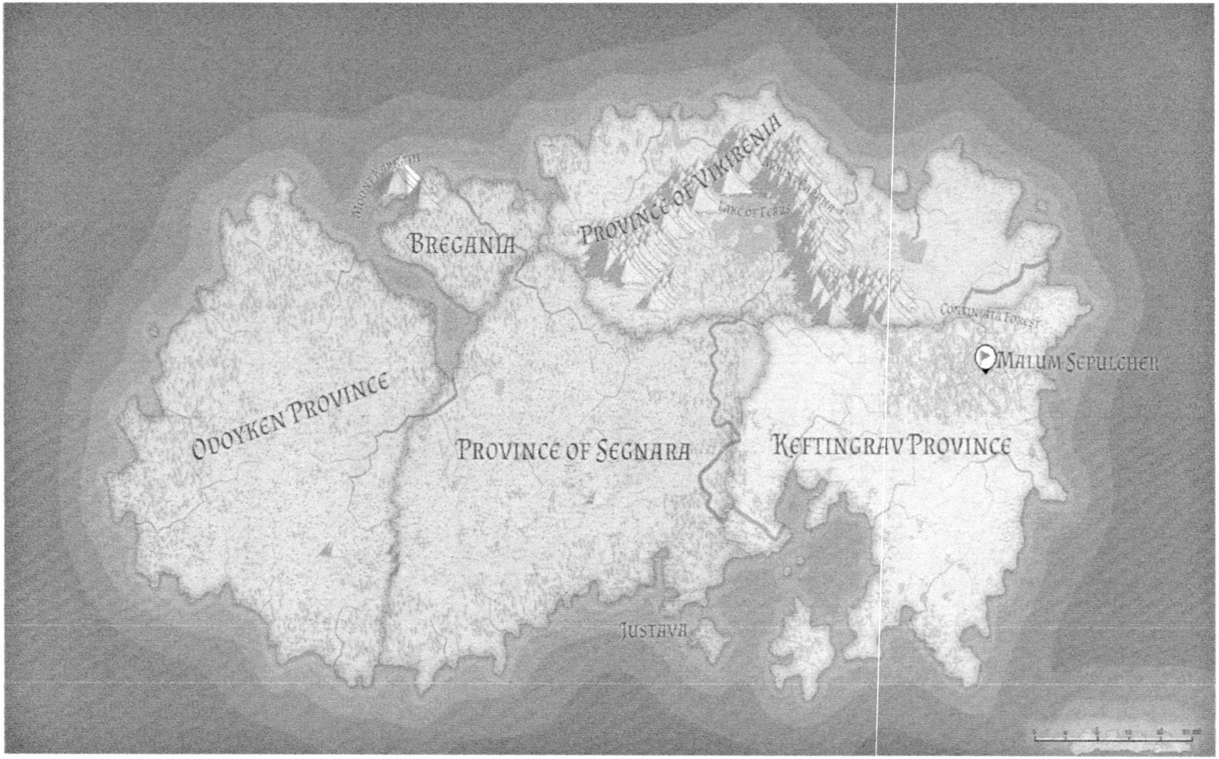

Odoyken Province
Bregania
Province of Vikirenia
Lake of Tears
Province of Segnara
Keftingrav Province
Malum Sepulcher
Justava

Part One

CHAPTER 1

THE CORONATION

(4th Era, Year 212)

It was a warm and sunny spring day in Gremela, the seas were shining, the magnolia and dogwood trees were in full bloom. The courtyard of the Castle on the Sea was filled with the citizens of Justava, who were watching as the workers erected a new white marble statue of the emperor to be.

Yojano was stepping in as emperor as his father was becoming a bit old. Yojano did not think his likeness on the statue was particularly great, but it was already done, hopefully it would grow on him. The Coronation was a wonderful event, there were trumpeters all around the courtyard, and a feast big enough to feed the whole city thrice over.

"Son, are you ready?" asked Yojano's father, Torano.

"As ready as I'll ever be Father," said a twenty-two-year-old Yojano nervously.

"Then we must begin" replied Torano.

Yojano's father turned and walked into the courtyard and began to speak to the people of Gremela.

"Citizens of Gremela, it is time I step down as emperor. Today, it is with great pride I pass the crown onto my son, Yojano. He is the youngest to ever be made emperor at just twenty-two years old, but fear not, he will lead you better than I am able." Just then, the two men standing at the base of the new statue pulled the large white sheet from it to reveal Yojano's statue, situated next to his own. The roar from the crowd was so loud the ground beneath their feet began to shake.

"Thank you all, my citizens. I will lead you all to the best of my ability until I can no longer." Said Yojano. "Please do help yourselves to the feast we have prepared, there is plenty to go around."

The citizens could not have been happier with the new emperor; if he was anything like his father, they all knew they were in good hands. The feasting and partying went on well into the night, and Yojano made sure to greet everyone personally. He felt that knowing the people you lead was the most important part of a successful leader.

Yojano made his way through the crowd at the end of the night in search of his father, who he found at the base of his own statue, situated next to his in the courtyard.

"Father, is everything okay?" Yojano asked.

"Yes, my son, I have led this empire for more than three decades. I have tried my best to lead the citizens of Gremela to greatness, but I fear I have many failures along the way." Replied Father, with a hint of sorrow in his voice. "I still cannot help but wonder if the evil that lived inside your brother was some fault of my own." Torano said as he gazed longingly at the night sky.

It seemed as if Torano's words took a long time to reach Yojano, who was also gazing up at the brilliantly lit night sky of Gremela. He stood next to his father and stared at the undulating reflection of the moons in the water for some time before he could think of anything to say.

"Father, what happened to Jeremiah?" Yojano asked, his voice full of curiosity.

Torano appeared slightly crestfallen, he leaned his elbows on the half wall in front of them and rested his hands in his face for a moment, as if thinking of exactly what to say.

"Son, I cannot answer that question truthfully. I do not know what happened to him. I saw signs of the evil that was within him since he was old enough to walk, I did my best to help him, tried to suppress it. There were times when I thought I was succeeding, but after the incident, I knew there was nothing more I could do." Said Torano, with a hint of regret in his voice. "I sent him to a school of sorts in the Isles of the West, a place that said they could help him."

Torano took a deep shuttering breath before continuing. Yojano looked horrified but was listening as closely as he could.

"I was receiving regular pixie deliveries and it seemed he was making great progress." Torano said as he took one more deep breath, as if telling the story was leaving him short of breath. "Until one day, I received a letter from the leader of the Isles of the West, telling me a large forest fire had broken out on the isle the school was on. They spent days searching what was left, they found no survivors." Torano said as he shed a tear in both eyes.

Yojano was dumbstruck, he did not know whether to believe his father. He found it hard to believe that his brother was gone. He had not seen him in many years, but he still found it hard to believe he was gone.

"Father, have you ever thought Jeremiah may have survived the fire, and simply ran away to safety?" asked Yojano.

"Oh, yes my son, I have. I asked the leader to search the isles for him, as they are a small empire, even smaller than us, and he to this day has seen no sign of him." Replied Torano. "My son, I think it is time we turn our attention to a more pressing matter"

Torano turned and began walking toward the castle doors, Yojano following closely behind him. They walked into Torano's quarters, and he sat down in the chair that Yojano sat in so often before. Noticing the puzzled look on Yojano's face, he motioned for him to sit down in the chair opposite him, the chair where the emperor sat. Yojano had almost forgotten that was his chair now, and after a minute, sat down upon it. At that moment, he felt a surge of righteous power and authority, he was not sure if it was the euphoria from recently being placed in charge, or if this was some sort of ancient Gremelan magic, but he enjoyed it nevertheless.

Upon sitting down, his father reached into his robes and pulled out a folded piece of parchment and handed it to him. Yojano gave his father an apprehensive look, but reached out and took the parchment. He sat back in his chair, unfolded the letter, and began to read.

Emperor Torano;

We believe we have found what you are looking for. Deep within the Continiata forest, there is a large white marble fountain with the bluest water we have ever seen. The water was..tempting. My brother could not resist, he drank some of the water. Upon drinking the water, the fountain lit up and a voice spoke to us, asking us what answers we sought. We asked the voice if it knew of a land across the endless sea.

The voice told us there was a land across the endless sea but would not tell us more unless we continued to drink. I cannot explain it, but I had a bad feeling, so we left at once. We are in the forest, surrounded by werewolves and other creatures whose power we know not, please send someone to help us.

The letter ended there. Yojano looked up at his father fearfully. Yojano had more than a few questions, it took him some time before he finally was able to ask one of them:

"Father, you sent these men into the forest in search of a new land across the Endless Sea?"

"Yes, and for a good reason my son. Gremela has seen nothing but peace for over two thousand years, ever since Mordon overthrew Mercado." Torano explained. "Many years ago, there was a story that told of Mercado's most faithful followers escaping on a ship across the endless sea, never to return. Some of us believe they found an uncharted island and have been living there, awaiting the return of Mercado."

"But Father, why is it that no one has gone looking for this island in all these years that have passed?" Yojano asked

"Oh my son but we have, there have been dozens of expeditions that led to nothing, and over half of them never returned. I knew my time as emperor was coming to an end and no attempt on my part was made to find this island. Many years ago, I heard rumors of a magical being living within the depths of the forest, that had answers to all questions. This magical being is who I sent them looking for, and it appears they have found it." Torano said with a look of excitement upon his face.

Yojano thought about what his father said for some time. He seemed troubled; he knew that this was going to be his responsibility now. He could not see why his father would chase something so insignificant. After a second thought he realized that finding this island was not insignificant, but more significant than anything he's ever had to do.

"So, what happens next?" Yojano asked his father.

"I should ask you that, my son. You are the emperor now." He replied.

Yojano had not thought of this, he was right, he was the emperor. These things were up to him now, but why would his father do half of this task and then pin the rest of it on him?

"What did you have in mind?" asked Yojano hopefully.

"I am glad you asked. There are two sailors here in Gremela, sailors I would consider the best in the empire. More than 20 years ago, it was these sailors that saved your grandfather and I from sinking in the western sea. The Mare Domitor had met its match that day."

Replied Torano, with a smile on his face. "If there are any sailors that could embark on this journey and emerge successful, it would be them, in this I have no doubt."

Yojano could hardly believe what he was hearing. Was his father really suggesting they send these two sailors across the endless sea in the hopes that they can find this land? It was the most foolish thing he had ever heard up to this point, but he suddenly remembered the importance of finding this land, to ensure the continued safety and peace within his empire. Yojano thought long and hard about this. If he did nothing, the inhabitants of the island could return, and that would be most problematic. But on the other hand, if he sent these two out, and they were successful, he could prevent the irreversible damage those men would inflict upon his empire.

"We shall do it" he said, making up his mind on the spot. Even though he made up his mind, he was less confident in his decision than before he made it. He let out a great sigh. "We will need to leave in the morning. Please ensure you get enough rest for the journey there." He said to his father, motioning for him to leave the room. Yojano spent the rest of the evening alone in his quarters, watching the light from the fire in the hearth flicker. His dreams were far from pleasant that night. One of them was of a ship catching fire in the middle of the ocean, another of the same ship being taken under by a giant unknown sea creature.

After a long and mostly sleepless night, Yojano was awoken by a ray of dazzling orange sunlight as the son crested over the horizon. The light hitting his face was exactly the motivation he needed to get out of bed and prepare for the journey ahead. He left his quarters and made his way down to the courtyard to watch the sunrise. The coastal Gremelan sunrise was a sight to behold, the sky was simply radiant with reds, oranges and yellows all blending and casting reflections on the deep blue waters.

Torano joined him a few minutes later and watched the sunrise in silence. They enjoyed each other's company for almost an hour before deciding it was time to head off. They turned on the spot and made their way down to the small dock that led them to the channel between the castle and mainland, sat down in one of the empty boats and rowed themselves to shore. The beach was empty aside from the two horses that were waiting for them.

"Father, where are we going?" asked Yojano.

"A small village, Galheim. In the Keftingrav Province." He replied.

"You said, you know these people?" Yojano asked "Do you think they will want to embark on this journey? It will likely lead to their disappearance, and we cannot pretend we don't know that." He warned his father.

"Of course not!" Torano said "If they do embark on this journey, it will likely only take a few months."

"But how? It's the *endless* sea, there is no end! They could sail for years!" Yojano interjected.

"Yojano, everything has an end. It's called the Endless Sea because only the most skilled of sailors can keep a bearing on those waters. Most ships end up sailing in circles for weeks or even months before making it out, and some ships never make it out."

Yojano seemed extremely troubled to hear this.

"So, what happens to them? The ones that never make it out I mean."

"We cannot be sure, they could still be sailing in circles, or they could have perished long ago, victims of the Endless Seas enormous swells."

There was silence for a while. Yojano seemed to be letting what his father just told him sink in. He was unsure how he felt about this. Were these sailors really that skilled? Could he really send two people out to sea on a potentially pointless journey? The journey they were taking would be the perfect time to let his thoughts consume him.

"Lead the way" said Yojano as he mounted his horse and motioned for his father to go in front of him. The two of them rode as far as they could in the beating sun before they stopped in a field that had a small lake with an outcropping of trees that blocked the scorching sunlight. They set up camp here for the night as they only had about a few hours of daylight left. Yojano went to the nearby lake and caught some Loxies while his father prepared and started the fire. They ate their fill of Loxies and fried apples before turning in for the night. Yojano laid in his makeshift bed watching the sun dip down beyond the horizon, and drifted off to sleep.

CHAPTER 2

GALHEIM

The next day in the early afternoon they came to a small lake just west of the border of Keftingrav. Torano dismounted his horse and took off all but his undergarments and went for a short swim in the lake. Yojano did the same as the early afternoon sun in spring was as fierce as it was bright.

After their swim they stopped to have some left over apples and some dried Loxie before continuing to Galheim. The Tower of Galheim could be seen on the eastern horizon. The tower was taller than any building in Gremela, second only to The Castle on the Sea. The tower itself was now in ruins and not usable, however it did serve as a great landmark when traveling east through Gremela as the tallest spire of the tower aligned perfectly with the Night Star, the brightest star in Gremela's night sky.

Yojano and his father were relieved to see the tower, this meant they would be in Galheim within the hour.

"Father, who are we meeting here?" asked Yojano.

"A man named Stromvir, and his wife Jarena. As I mentioned before, they saved your grandfather and I from sinking on the western sea more than twenty years ago." Replied Father.

Yojano paused and thought about what his father told him for a moment before continuing with his questions.

"What makes you think they will even agree to this? A far from pleasant journey lies ahead should they agree." Yojano said matter-of-factly.

"I would tend to agree with you, we may need to offer them something in return." Torano replied, a look of deep contemplation lined his face as he said this. Yojano knew he was right, they would need to offer them something in return, something that would make this journey worth their while.

They arrived at Galheim at last and received a very warm welcome. Rows and rows of people were bowing as they passed through, muttering praises about the emperor to themselves all the while. Yojano and his father dismounted and continued on foot, stopping to talk to anyone who wanted before continuing on to find Stromvir.

Galheim was quite beautiful. The streets were lined with magnolia and lilac trees, the whole city smelled of cedar as that is what the houses and buildings were made of, not to mention the entire city wall was lined with cedar trees.

They followed the main road almost to the end and turned down a small road to the left and made their way deeper into the city. After a long walk, they came to a house that was different than all the rest. It was made of stone and mostly covered in moss.

"Let them be here" muttered Torano as he started to knock on the door.

He knocked on the door and a few moments later a tall man with a scruffy beard and straight shoulder length black hair answered the door.

"Emperor! What a pleasant surprise! What brings you here?" asked Stromvir.

Stromvir looked at Torano and could tell by the look on his face that this was not a leisurely visit, but something far more serious. He ushered them inside and closed the door behind them. He grabbed a decanter of wine and three glasses and began pouring for all of them.

Once they all sat Torano began to speak.

"How are you doing, Stromvir? It has been far too long."

"We are doing what we can I must say. Times are a little tough for us right now." Stromvir said as he bowed his head in shame.

"Stromvir, there is nothing to be ashamed of. It can happen to anyone at any time." Replied Torano as he placed a reassuring hand on Stromvir's shoulder.

Stromvir looked up at Torano hopefully, and before long a short black-haired woman with blazingly bright blue eyes came into the room holding a small child in her arms. She placed the child on the floor, and he began to play with a small pile of wooden blocks that were scattered about.

"Emperor Torano!" she exclaimed "How are you? And who is this with you? It can't be Yojano!"

"Aye, but it is Yojano, and he is the one you call emperor now" Torano replied.

"It's a pleasure, Jarena, is it?" Yojano asked as he bowed his head and gave her a kiss on the hand. Her face suddenly flushed with color as she returned a courteous bow. Yojano could tell they were both nervous to meet him, but he assured them there was nothing to be nervous about, he was just a person like everyone else.

After a few minutes that seemed like hours of small talk, Torano reminded everyone of why they came in the first place. He pulled out the letter they received and placed it on the table in front of Stromvir and Jarena. They hesitated for a few moments before reaching out and unfolding the parchment slowly. Stromvir and Jarena read the letter and set it down on the table in front of him and let out a great sigh.

"I know what you're thinking Torano but we can't. We have him now, we have Jareth. What are we supposed to do about him? We surely cannot take him with us, he is not even two years old." Stromvir explained.

"We will provide you with the *Mare Domitor*" said Torano. Torano went on to explain of the possibility that the inhabitants of the island could be remnants of

Mercado's regime, and that first contact must be made as soon as possible.

Stromvir's demeanor suddenly changed.

"I thought the *Mare Domitor* was destroyed more than a decade ago?" asked Stromvir inquisitively.

"That is what we wished the empire at large to believe. It is well hidden on the western coast of Gremela." Torano said

Stromvir and Jarena were looking at each other with great concern and wonder on their faces. Yojano could tell they were trying to communicate their thoughts to one another. He had a feeling they were coming up with all the reasons why they could not embark on this journey. It was at that moment that Yojano thought of something.

"If I may say something, you and your husband have provided my family with a debt we can never repay when you saved my father's and grandfather's life all those years ago. Should you embark on this journey, you and your family will always have a place in the Castle on the Sea. You would be doing Gremela a great service, a service that cannot be repaid by even this, but it is all I can offer you at this time" Yojano said hopefully.

Stromvir and Jarena appeared taken aback, unsure of how to respond to the offer. This was something they needed, especially now that they had a young son they had to care for. Several minutes passed in silence before anyone spoke again.

"We understand that the journey will be nothing short of treacherous. That is why we chose you, after watching you and Jarena save my father and I from our sinking ship, there is no one else I trust with this. The *Mare Domitor* is yours now. I have no use for it anymore, and neither will Yojano." Replied Torano.

"We will do it. When do we leave?" asked Jarena.

"Jarena! We must discuss this, what about Jareth?" asked Stromvir.

"Your brother will watch after him, will he not? " asked Jarena.

"Of course he will, but who knows how long we will be gone." Said Stromvir.

Jarena turned to address Yojano.

"Sir, how long do you think this will take?"

"We cannot be sure, but it should not take any longer than a few months." Torano answered. Yojano seemed relieved that his father answered the question and not him. Torano went on to explain to them about the endless sea not really being endless.

"The thought alone nearly kills me, but what happens if something happens to us?" Asked Stromvir

"Well, I cannot foresee that happening. You shall have the Mare Domitor after all!" Torano said with a chuckle.

Yojano interrupted.

"My father is very good at not answering questions that are asked of him if you couldn't tell. Should something happen to the two of you, I will personally ensure the safety of your son. I however, can only do so until he is an adult, after that I am afraid the protection I can offer will lapse." Said Yojano, he could tell that his was what Jarena wanted to hear, and suddenly, the demeanor in the room shifted once more.

Yojano could tell they needed some time to think about this. He patted his father on the shoulder and motioned for them to leave.

"We will give the two of you some time. We shall return in the morning" he said before walking out the door, his father in tow. The two of them walked in the woods surrounding Stromvir's house until they came to a suitable clearing for a camp. They set up camp and packed it in for the day, knowing they would need to be up at first light the following morning.

"What do you think?" asked Torano, looking at Yojano.

"Think?" Yojano replied

"Of them, do you think they will do it?"

"I cannot be sure; they have a young son. I think it would be unwise, but whatever decision they make, we must respect it." Yojano said assertively. "We have left the decision up to them, should they choose not to, we will need to make other arrangements."

"Yes, I agree." Torano said as he nodded in agreement with his son. They sat around their fire for a while thinking of the journey that lies ahead, not just for them, but for everyone. This journey would affect every living being in Gremela whether they knew it or not.

Back in the house, Stromvir and Jarena were not taking this decision lightly. They too were aware of the impact this journey would have on the people of Gremela, successful or not. Stromvir sat with his face in his hands for a while, Jarena clinging on to his shoulder in comfort. They knew what they had to do, but how could they? How could they leave their only son? If Yojano kept his word, they would be permitted to raise Jareth in the Castle on the Sea. They would have no need to worry about food or shelter again. There were more than enough rooms in the Castle on the Sea. Stromvir figured they could live there and likely never see any of the other inhabitants, due to the vastness of the castle.

Jarena walked over to the place on the floor where Jareth was playing with his blocks. He was building them up and knocking them over again and again, expelling a loud giggle every time the tower he built would topple. Stromvir and Jarena sat and watched him play for a while in admiration. It was clear they were not taking the decision they were making lightly.

The following morning Yojano and Torano returned to the small house in the woods just as they promised. Stromvir poured each of them a bowl of porridge and filled their goblets with some oak mead before joining them at the table. There was a brilliant fire lit in the fireplace over which a couple of freshly caught Loxies were cooking. Everyone sat down at the table, including Jareth who was sitting on Jarena's lap, giving all his attention to the brightly colored berries on the table.

"Well, your continued presence here leads me to believe you are willing to embark on this journey. Am I correct?" asked Yojano after they all sat down.

"You are, sir." Replied Stromvir.

"I am glad." Yojano replied. "We shall see you in a few days. You'll need this."

Yojano handed Stromvir a small map of the western coast of Gremela. Stromvir saw the spot where they were to meet, it was circled in black ink with the words "Port of Mare" scrawled above it in hasty looking handwriting.

CHAPTER 3

THE JOURNEY AHEAD

Stromvir and Jarena were feeling a mixture of emotions with respect to the journey that lay ahead. They were both anxious, excited, fearful, and yet brave at the same time. They were most concerned for their son Jareth, who was young and unable to understand what was happening. Stromvir put great trust in his brother, he could trust no one else with the care of his son.

Jarena was especially worried, she did not want to leave her son, but she knew this mission was far too important. They would have to succeed in their mission as quickly as they could and come back to get their son.

Stromvir and Jarena were packing their belongings into their packs and getting ready to set out for the Mare Domitor, they would be meeting Yojano and his father there in five days' time. They needed to travel to Drahmstar to explain to Stromvir's brother what they were doing, and to ask a great favor of him. Luckily for them the location of the Mare Domitor was close by, just one day's trip from Drahmstar.

"Strom, we need to make sure we finish this journey as quickly as possible! Is it impossible to take Jareth with us?" Jarena said as tears dripped down her face.

"Jareth will be safest in the hands of Dravin, there is no other way. Yojano assured me that no matter what happens, Jareth will be well cared for." Stromvir reassured Jarena.

"Have you considered that your brother might refuse?" asked Jarena cautiously.

"I have, but if I know my brother as I think I do, he will gladly accept. We have always looked out for one another" Stromvir said.

"I hope you are correct, otherwise we may be forced to take him with us, or just simply refuse the journey" Jarena stated as she finished getting their horses ready and carriage packed.

When they were finished getting all the supplies needed, they met with Yojano and his father one last time.

"We shall be off within the hour" stated Stromvir. "We will meet you in five days' time"

With that, the four of them mounted up, Jareth riding in the carriage. Thus they began their separate journeys. The next day Yojano and his father were camped not far from Galheim. Torano pulled out the letter from the two messengers he sent out. He needed to go to the forest and look for them, he could not just leave them out there.

"Son, we need to go to the Continiata forest, it is only a half a day away. We have at least two days head start, as they will need that time to drop off their son and travel to us." Said Torano.

"Father, I think going to the forest at the present time would be unwise. We shall wait until we send Stromvir and Jarena off." Yojano said.

"Son, I can't leave those men behind. I'll be leaving at first light." Replied Torano

"No, you will not. I am Emperor, and you may be my father, but I am still emperor, and if you want me to start acting like an emperor, you should start treating me like an emperor" said Yojano sternly

"You are right." replied Torano

"Thank you, now we must eat something before we head out." Said Yojano "We shall go to the forest after the ship has sailed, we can even stop by the castle and get a few more men should we require them" stated Yojano.

"It was foolish of me to think we could go to the forest now, we need to prepare before we go into the forest. We will send them off then to look for my men" said Torano hesitantly.

Upon arriving at the ship's location Yojano became very confused, they were standing at the edge of a very small pond. It was barely big enough for a small rowboat to fit.

"Father, this is a mere pond! You mean to tell me the Mare Domitor is here?" questioned Yojano.

"Of course not. Let me show you" replied Torano.

Torano took off his boots and pulled up the bottom of his trousers so they would not get wet, and he stepped into the water. He motioned for Yojano to follow him. Yojano followed him to the center of the pond where he could see something just beneath the surface of the water, it looked like an old lamp post. Torano told Yojano to head out through the trees to the sea. After Yojano left, Torano reached down into the water with both hands and turned the top of the lamp post hard to the left until it made a loud clicking sound.

Just then, as Yojano was standing on the beach he felt the ground beneath him start to shake, this was about the time his father came and stood next to him on the beach. Within a few moments, they could both see the water of the sea start to bubble up, as if something was coming up from the bottom.

"Father, what is happening?" asked Yojano seriously.

"You shall see, any moment now." Replied Torano.

Just then a loud *woosh* came from the ocean as something started to emerge from underneath the surface. Before Yojano had a moment to fully grasp what was happening, he saw the top of the mast of a great ship, the biggest ship he had ever seen. As it rose out of the water and seemed to never fully emerge, Yojano realized just how large this ship was.

The ship finally emerged from the water, and it was magnificent. The Mare Domitor was like no other ship Yojano had seen before. There were three masts, one of which was the main mast, as it was the tallest of the three. The total length of the ship exceeded four hundred feet, which included the length of the bow sprit at the front of the ship, which was over fifty feet long itself.

The rudder was controlled by an immense wooden wheel on deck of the ship. The hull and deck of the ship were made of Brickon wood, an incredibly strong wood indigenous to the Continiata Forest. Each mast of the ship was made from a trunk of a felled Brickon tree and was sunk down into the keel of the ship, to prevent the snapping of the mast.

"Father, this is the biggest ship I have ever seen. When was this built?" Yojano inquired.

"I cannot answer that. I was given the ship by my father, and he by his father, and he by his, and so on for as long as our family history is recorded." Said Torano. "It was used in one of the last battles against Mercado, and your grandfather and I used it to explore the endless sea almost thirty years ago."

"Stromvir and Jarena will need a crew to sail this properly, do we have a crew for them?" asked Yojano.

"Of course. Follow me." Torano replied as he began to wade into the water.

Yojano followed his father into the water, wading his way out to the ship. When they made it to the side of the ship a rope ladder fell from the side as if someone atop the ship had kicked it down. Perplexed though he was, Yojano climbed up the ladder and onto the deck of the immense ship. The ship was mesmerizing. Everything on the ship was painted to perfection and perfectly symmetrical. The top deck of the ship was equipped with an immense wooden wheel which had gold and silver inlays all over it. The crow's nest had a small ladder leading up to it and a long narrow pole for sliding down. Yojano was in disbelief. He had never seen anything like this before. A ship bigger than he had ever seen before just came out from under the ocean, he was beyond words.

"Father, how is this ship even possible? How was it under water?"

"This ship has been around since before Mercado was defeated. Magic was everywhere in Gremela back then. If I am not mistaken, this is the only relic of that time that has maintained the magic it was built with after all this time." Torano replied. "Come on, there is much to see."

Yojano followed his father through a little door that was beneath the helm of the ship. Upon entering

Yojano's jaw almost hit the floor. Inside the hull of the ship was a grand room lined with tables and chairs and beds and everything of the like. These were the most sophisticated pieces of furniture Yojano had ever seen. Large wooden statues of all the previous captains and crew of the ship lined the walls from floor to ceiling. There must have been at least one hundred statues surrounding the room. They continued to the other end of the large room and approached another door which contained a set of steps leading down to the lower level of the ship. The main room of the lower deck had small round port holes lining either side, with rows of benches in between. In the middle of each bench sat two wooden gargoyle statues, perfectly aligned and each unique. Yojano assumed this to be the room the crew would row from should the ship's sails break. Next to this room was a massive empty room, usually used as a cargo hold, and on the far end of the cargo hold, there was a singular room with iron bars surrounding it. Undoubtedly the brig, a place to separate any unruly crewmen.

Torano was standing opposite the brig, facing a wall that contained a bookshelf full of books. Torano approached the bookshelf and began removing various books, and after five had been removed, the ship shook violently as though it had been attacked. At once Yojano turned and ran up the stairs, his father close behind him.

"Do not worry Yojano, I intended this." He said as they continued up the stairs. When they reemerged into the main hall of the ship, Yojano was left completely speechless. One by one, the great statues of the past captains and crew were coming to life before their very eyes. The statues on the top row were jumping from their plinths and landing on the floor below, kneeling before their captain, ready to serve.

"Man your positions!" Torano shouted.

All the statues turned and in a single file line, marched in unison up to the top deck. The four statues closest to them marched past them and down into the lower deck. Yojano crossed the large room, following closely behind the marching statues. On the deck, each statue was performing a different task, there was a group of them preparing the sails, another group was counting the rations, there was one statue climbing up to the crow's nest. The statues went about their business for some time while Yojano and his father made their way back to land to set up camp before nightfall. Stromvir and Jarena would be meeting them the day after next, so they needed to make sure everything was ready for their arrival.

"The ship will be ready to embark by morning, the crew works quickly." Said Torano.

Yojano was still at a loss for words, he never knew Gremela had magic, let alone ever seeing it to this extent.

"What happened to the magic in Gremela, father?" he asked.

"I do not know the whole story son, your grandfather died before he could pass that information on to me. I believe we both shall find out more in due time." Torano replied. "Let's get some sleep, we have a long day ahead of us tomorrow and the next."

The sun was cresting over the horizon and slowly dipping out of sight. Yojano laid awake for a while thinking of everything he had seen today. The magical properties of the ship gave him hope that maybe they would make it after all, perhaps, it was not a suicide mission. Perhaps, there was something more to the journey Yojano did not know.

CHAPTER 4

A TALE OF TWO BROTHERS

Stromvir left the encampment in search of a suitable fishing spot. A couple of freshly caught Loxies would make for an excellent dinner for him and his family. He cast his poles out and sat by the water, watching the sun slowly set. He knew he had a little over an hour of daylight left, so he knew he needed to catch some quickly so he could get them cooked and served to his family. He caught a few, and he was under the impression that he might have hooked another when suddenly a man almost a foot taller than him came out from the trees behind him. The man appeared disoriented and possibly hurt.

"Are you okay sir?" inquired Stromvir.

"..no..can barely..walk..need…" said the man before he collapsed onto the ground at Stromvir's feet. Stromvir heaved the unconscious man over his shoulder and started back towards the camp when he heard a noise coming from the trees, it was another man, presumably a friend of the unconscious man over Strom's shoulders. The friend was also injured and disoriented.

"Sir, where did you find that man?" asked the stranger.

"He walked out of the very same woods you did and collapsed in front of me. I asked if he was okay, but he stammered over a few words before falling over" replied Stromvir.

"I've got a camp not even a mile from here, I can take you there. I can cook you up some of these Loxies I caught not even an hour ago, there's plenty to go around."

"Thanks. Name's Reo, and that's my brother Kol. We were completing a task the emperor sent us on and we somehow ended up here. We were in the Continiata Forest last we knew. Where are we now? Looks like the western coast." Asked Reo.

"We are in the Odoyken Province, how did you get all the way out here? The whole empire stretches in between the two places." Said Stromvir, puzzled.

"We cannot say. It just happened, like it was magic" Reo responded. "We woke up here. The Emperor sent us out to the forest in search of something. Even he was unsure exactly what we were looking for." Reo said. "We spent a few days slowly making our way through the thick forest. Our canteens had been empty for more than a day, were thirsty, hungry, and disoriented. Truth be told, we realized we were lost after the first day. We wanted to turn back, but we weren't even sure which way back was."

Stromvir was listening intently, he noticed the unconscious brother on the ground stirred for a moment, then fell limp once more.

"You must have found something, surely?" asked Stromvir.

"We did. We finally came to a small clearing within the dense forest. There was a white marble fountain, which contained the purest and bluest water we had ever seen. It was almost, mesmerizing. My brother could not resist the temptation, and drank some of the water to quench his thirst." Reo continued "Upon drinking, the voice of a man spoke to us, asking us what answers we sought."

"A voice spoke to you?" Stromvir asked skeptically.

"I am sorry, I cannot explain it. It was like magic. We asked if there was a land across the endless sea."

Stromvir's eyes widened, this could be the answer. Perhaps the man standing before him knew how to get to the land he was setting sail for in just a few days.

"What did the voice tell you?" asked Stromvir

"It told us there was a land across the endless sea, but the exact location could not be revealed to us until I drank from the fountain as well." Reo said, a fearful look in his eyes. "At that moment, my brother fell over and began to convulse. The voice became sinister, almost evil. It began demanding us to stay. The voice was frantic, desperate. I picked up my brother and threw him over my shoulder and ran out of there as fast I could."

Stromvir was horror stricken. He had never heard of such a thing, and never knew anyone that had either. He knew the emperor ought to hear this.

"Is there anything else?" asked Stromvir.

"As we were leaving, the voice was demanding we stay, telling us we would regret leaving." Reo said. "I ran as fast and as far as I could. I could hear the howls of the werewolves closing in on us. I kept running, darkness began to shroud us, I could barely see my hand in front of my face. The howls of the werewolves were getting closer. Eventually I could not continue, I needed rest. I put my brother on the ground and before I could do anything, I fell to the ground. That is the last thing I remember; I woke up shortly after just beyond where you found us."

"I think you should tell the emperor about this. I will be meeting him in a few days. Let's go to my camp." Stromvir said.

Stromvir helped Reo carry his unconscious brother back to the camp. They all began tending to him at once, ensuring he had water and some food in case he woke up. Reo was desperately hungry as well, he was relieved when Stromvir told him to eat as much as he wanted. Reo felt slightly guilty about this, but it appeared there was more than enough food to go around, at least for the time being.

Stromvir and Jarena were tending to Kol when Reo stepped outside for a moment. He was looking out at the sea, thinking of the events that had just transpired. Suddenly, his mind filled with rage, the emperor he had been faithful to for so long had sent him to his certain death. He was beginning to let his thoughts get away from him when he was startled by the sudden appearance of Stromvir at his side.

"Where are you meeting the emperor?" Reo asked.

"At a small port one day's journey away. We are traveling to the nearby village tomorrow morning. We have something we must attend to." Stromvir said. "The two of you are more than welcome to come along. But if you wish to part ways, I shall not stop you."

"Thank you, Stromvir. Your kindness is appreciated. I shall stay with my brother tomorrow." Reo said

"We will come back here once we are done in the village to help take camp down before we set off." Stromvir responded. "There is plenty of room in our wagon for you and your brother."

"Thank you, Stromvir." Reo responded as he walked back into the tent to see his brother lying there, looking better than before. It looked as though he was going to be okay.

"He shall be okay." Said Jarena reassuringly. "Now, please. Tell me what happened. I know you have told Stromvir, but I would like to hear as well, if you please."

Reo took one deep shuddering breath and retold the whole story of what happened to them. He left out no details, making sure every part of the story was retold to the best of his ability, he could not help but feel part of his story was missing. He simply could not understand how he woke up on the other side of the empire, but seemingly in the same place he was when he passed out.

Jarena's face seemed filled with horror, she shuddered when each time he mentioned the werewolves, it was obvious she was fearful of them.

"You guys must tell the emperor about this." said Jarena.

"We will, Stromvir has offered to let us come along." Reo replied.

"Well, it's settled then." Said Jarena happily. "It is getting late; I think it's best if we all got some sleep."

The next day when Stromvir woke up, he, Jarena and Jareth made their way to the village. The ride to the village was silent, both Stromvir and Jarena had nothing to say. They were starting to regret their decision. Perhaps Strom's brother would not agree to look after Jareth in their absence. If that happened, they would have no choice but to tell the emperor they could not be the ones to set sail.

The village was small and comprised of small houses on one side and a large pasture on the other side. The residents of the village operated a farm to help feed themselves. It was a community effort, residents worked in shifts to tend to the gardens and the animals they raised. The houses were made mostly from wood and reinforced with stone. The roofs were made of hardened clay gathered from a nearby clay deposit. All the houses had a singular chimney, most of which seemed to be constantly blowing smoke from the top.

At the end of the row of houses there was a path leading into a small outcropping of woods just within shouting distance. At the end of the path there was a small clearing. In the clearing there was a small wooden house, however it was slightly bigger than all the rest. There was a large firepit with a pig roasting over it, the entire clearing smelled of it.

The door to the small house creaked open, and a man who bore a striking resemblance to Stromvir stood in the doorway.

"Strom?" The man questioned. "What are you doing here?"

"Dravin, my brother. It's been a long time". Stromvir said.

"It sure has! What brings you all the way out here?" asked Dravin while motioning for everyone to come inside.

Upon entering the house Stromvir realized that Dravin understood the severity of the situation. He got out a bottle of mead and poured glasses for everyone.

"To what do I owe this pleasure, brother?" asked Dravin seriously.

Stromvir looked at his brother with a mixture of fear and excitement in his eyes. Dravin knew his life was about to change for a while.

"Brother, we must ask a favor of you. It is one we have not thought about lightly." Said Stromvir.

"Well, let us hear it, Strom." Said Dravin as he let out an exasperated sigh.

"The emperor, the new Emperor, Yojano and his father Torano came to visit us in Galheim. They have informed us of some information they received and want us to go on a journey. They have received word that there is an undiscovered land across the endless sea. The

Emperor has prepared the Mare Domitor for us to use along with a sizeable crew." Explained Stromvir.

"I see, well brother, where do I come into this?" asked Dravin.

Stromvir's face dropped, he put his hands in his lap and stood up. He walked out the door to their carriage and retrieved his young son. He reentered the house and immediately Dravin knew what was going to be asked of him.

"Strom, you're not asking what I think you're asking are you?" questioned Dravin.

"We will be back as soon as we can, but we will be gone for far too long to take him with us. The sea is no place for a young boy." Said Stromvir

The expression on Dravin's face was a clear indicator of what he thought about the proposal. He looked as if he had just received some terrible news.

"Strom, I haven't any idea what to say. How long will you be gone?" asked Dravin.

"Shouldn't be any longer than a few months."

Stromvir leaned in close to his brother, as if to whisper a secret in his ear.

"The emperor has promised us a place within the castle on the sea for as long as we live should we embark on this journey. I shall see to it that you are included in that as well." Stromvir said as he placed his hand on his brother's shoulder reassuringly.

Dravin's demeanor suddenly changed; it was almost as if he was suddenly happy about the task given to him.

"When are you setting sail?"

Stromvir took this to mean that his brother accepted. He felt as though a heavy weight dropped from his shoulders, and he hugged his brother with such ferocity he almost knocked him over.

"The day after tomorrow, but we must head out tonight to meet the emperor" said Stromvir, relinquishing his tight grip on his brother.

It was hard to tell what Dravin was thinking. The expression on his face was blank, yet solid. Stromvir did not know what to think, but he knew his brother would take good care of his son.

Jarena sobbed endlessly as she said goodbye to her son, she was heartbroken, but she knew her love would protect him and keep him from harm until she could return to him. She knew Yojano would keep him safe. She told him she loved him, scooped him up in her arms and gave him a hug that everyone thought would never end. She set Jareth down on the wolfskin rug on the floor, with three wooden blocks and a wooden ball Stromvir had made for him. These were his favorite toys.

Stromvir knelt on the rug next to his son and put his hand on his shoulder. He told him he loved him, and that he would be back soon. He told him to listen to his uncle and to always remember that he would come back for him. Jareth looked up at Stromvir with a smile, and a tear slid down Stromvir's face as he gave his son one last hug and ruffled the hair on his head. With that, Stromvir and Jarena were out the door and headed back to their carriage and soon enough, were out of sight.

They rode to meet the emperor in complete silence. They knew what they were doing was foolish, but they also knew they had to do it. No one else was capable and it was crucial to the empire that they be the ones to discover the new land first. They spent the night thinking about what lay ahead of them. It was almost morning when they arrived at the spot they had discussed with the emperor. Reo and Stromvir set up a small camp by fire light. Reo and his brother were sleeping in the tent, the others in the carriage. There were only a few hours until dawn, but they all decided to get some sleep nonetheless, the emperor would be meeting them in the morning. Stromvir laid awake for some time, thinking he could hear something outside the carriage, but after a long silence he convinced himself his lack of sleep was making him imagine things.

Dawn was just about to break on the horizon when Stromvir was awoken by a loud sound. Startled, he quickly got up to find what had happened. Not more than one hundred yards from where they were, he saw Reo on his knees hitting something on the ground repeatedly. Stromvir ran over to see what it was and when he got there, he was mortified. Reo had found Torano's quarters, pulled him out of bed, and knocked him around. Stromvir realized he must have heard Torano and Yojano arriving in the distance just a few hours previous.

"Stop! Stop! Reo let him up now!" Bellowed Stromvir

"You sent us to die! You abandoned us!" He yelled as he continued to rain his fists down on any part of Torano's body he could hit.

"REO!" Stromvir yelled as he tackled Reo, and almost without a pause, Reo was back up and headed for

Torano again. Stromvir again was able to tackle and pin him down.

"Yojano!" Stromvir yelled as Reo struggled beneath him, pinned by Stromvir's right foot.

Just then, some leaves from a nearby bush began to rustle, and shortly after Yojano came stumbling out of the bushes and upon seeing his father bloodied and laying on the ground, turned to Stromvir and Reo.

"Your Majesty, I found this one on top of your father when I woke up. He did this." Said Stromvir.

"Yes! And I would do it again given the chance after what he did to us" exclaimed Reo.

Yojano walked up to where they were standing and motioned for Stromvir to release him. Reo stood up and came face to face with Yojano before finally breaking the silence.

"Who are you?" Reo said as his face went from angry to fearful.

"I should be the one asking you that, considering you just beat my father half to death." Replied Yojano, his eyes fixated on Reo's with an unyielding stillness.

"The emperor sent us out there to die, and he knew it all along!" replied Reo whose face had once again turned angry.

"I'm the emperor. My father handed me the throne not more than a month ago. Now, would you mind helping us get him up? I think it's the least you can do after all. You'll join me in my quarters after." Said Yojano as he patted Reo's shoulder and gave him a small half smile as he began kneeling to help his father.

Reo did as he was told and as he expected, was doing most of the work, even he agreed this was fair considering the circumstances. Reo began to feel that Yojano had purposely taken the long way to get wherever it was they were going.

"Just over here, past this tree!" Said Yojano as they came around a tree they had passed several times into a small camp. "I think I may have been lost there for a second" said Yojano as he winked at Reo and chuckled to himself.

Everyone followed Yojano into the camp and laid his father down inside his quarters. Jarena came around with water and some rags for him. They cleaned him up and gave him the water, he laid there for about an hour before waking up.

"Father, are you okay?" asked Yojano.

"I'm okay son, what happened?" asked Torano.

"I acted on impulse, sir. I apologize. I can never hope to repay the damage I have caused." Reo said. Yojano was impressed with Reo admitting fault, and not trying to cast blame on his father.

"Reo, what happened out there?" asked Torano.

Reo explained everything that had happened, and everyone was shocked and confused, wondering what happened to Kol out there.

"Well, it sounds like Stromvir and Jarena may actually succeed." Said Torano.

"Succeed in what?" asked Reo.

"Well, they have agreed to sail across the endless sea in search of the land this voice spoke of." Replied Torano.

"Sir, that's impossible, it's a death sentence!" yelled Reo.

"I have the utmost faith in them, they saved me once while I was out there, I have no reason to think they should not conquer that sea again. Especially with the aid of the Mare Domitor." Replied Torano.

"The Mare Domitor?" Reo responded inquisitively.

"Their ship, it's over there." Torano said as he pointed toward the sea, which had the largest ship Reo had ever seen anchored just offshore.

"I am sure Stromvir and Jarena would enjoy the company. I believe these two shall go with them." Yojano said.

"Sir?" Reo questioned.

"I think they could make good use of you, don't you?" Yojano winked as he asked his father.

"I am sure they would make excellent use of them, after everything they have been through, it seems only right they get to help discover the land once and for all" Torano said.

"It would be a pleasure; we will help in any way we can." Reo said. He made his way back to the camp and back into the tent where his brother lay, stirring.

"We set sail tomorrow, brother."

CHAPTER 5

ABOARD THE MARE DOMITOR

After a long and hard night's sleep Stromvir awoke before everyone else just before dawn. He hiked up to a small cliff overlooking the ocean he was about to sail into, the sun was rising behind him, making the water glisten with a red and orange hue. There was a group of kingfishers down below, diving to retrieve quite the collection of small Loxies.

He sat on the edge of the cliff for more than an hour, picturing the journey ahead. He knew it would be no easy task, as he had not sailed a ship in more than ten years, it might take a little while to regain his sea legs. He could see the camp from where he was, he looked down to see that just about everyone was awake. Some were having a meal, some were preparing belongings, and the members of the crew were already on board the ship preparing it for the voyage.

He made his way back down to the camp, where everyone was apparently looking for him. He walked for a few minutes when he came across the emperor talking to Kol and Reo.

"I have said what I said, and that is the end of it. I expect to hear nothing further from either of you on this matter." Yojano said as he turned to walk away, only to be stopped by Stromvir.

"Ah, hello Stromvir. How are you?" Yojano asked as they began walking towards his quarters.

"As good as I can be, sir." Replied Stromvir with a little hesitation in his voice.

"Excellent" He said. "Follow me, I think it's time you see your new ship."

They all walked to the edge of the beach where the rowboat was waiting for them. They all clambered into the rowboat that was clearly meant for two people and began making their way to the ship.

"Your crew has already begun preparations for the journey." Yojano said.

"Excellent, where did you find the crew?" Stromvir asked inquisitively.

"You will see, this ship is quite something." Yojano said with a smirk.

Upon arriving at the boat, once again the rope ladder fell in front of them as if someone dropped it from above. One by one they climbed up the ladder, Stromvir was the last one to climb on, and when he did the ladder began to pull itself up to the deck where it previously was coiled up. This startled Stromvir, causing him to slip slightly, but he gathered himself and climbed onto the main deck when he reached the top. He and Jarena had never seen anything like this before. The ship was magnificent, it looked as though it were just built. The wood still shined, the helm was spotless, and the sails were a pristine white. They both looked around the ship, taking everything in, when Stromvir noticed a member of the crew passing in front of him. He believed he had gone mad; he was sure the crewman that just passed in front of him was made of wood. He was beginning to ask a question when it was answered for him.

"Yes, they are made of wood. Brickon wood, same as the ship." Yojano said, stifling a chuckle.

"How are they..? I have never seen anything quite like this, sir." Stromvir said, Jarena agreeing.

"This ship was built long ago, during a time when magic was abundant, we believe it is the only relic that retained its magical properties after all these years." Yojano said. "Even we are unsure of its full capabilities, we hope you will uncover more."

"Who are they?" Stromvir asked.

"These are the past crewmen and captains of the ship. They and they alone know the secrets this ship holds" said Yojano.

Stromvir was in awe of what he was seeing. He was eager to see more of the ship. Yojano and his father began walking toward the door situated underneath the helm, the door that led to the room where the statues had been standing dormant for decades. Stromvir and Jarena followed Yojano and his father through the ship, examining every part of the main hall in detail. After about an hour that seemed only a few minutes, they descended into the cargo hold.

In the depths of the cargo hold Torano began showing Stromvir how to return the statues to their plinths. He showed them the brig, and how to lock and unlock the cell, and finally he showed them the rowing room. The room in which the crew would come to row the boat ashore should something happen to the sails of the ship. They returned to the top deck and were shown the outer workings of the ship. They made their way around the ship and eventually up to the helm. Torano gestured for Stromvir to take his place in front of the helm, which he did hesitantly.

"Take care of her, Captain."

At that very moment, all the crewmen stopped what they were doing, faced Stromvir, and bowed before him, ready to serve. One of them walked up to him and stuck out his hand.

"Pleasure to meet you, Captain" said the wooden man. He was taller than Stromvir, had a long beard with a curled mustache, and thick hair. His voice sounded like what you would expect a man made from wood to sound like.

"The pleasure is all mine." Stromvir stated as he smiled and shook his hand. The man had a rather firm grip, so much so that even a man as stout as Stromvir was slightly taken aback. Stromvir and Jarena continued to examine their new ship and made small conversations with random members of the crew. Yojano noticed his father walking back inside the main hull of the ship, keen to see what he was up to, Yojano followed.

When he made his way into the main room of the ship, he saw his father at the other end of the room, seated at the end of a large wooden table. Yojano walked across the room and sat down opposite his father.

"Yojano, please go and bring Stromvir to me. I have one last thing to attend to." Torano requested.

Yojano went to retrieve Stromvir, they needed to have a final word with him before he set off. Torano reached into his rucksack and pulled out an object that was wrapped delicately in a white cloth and placed it on the table in front of them. As Stromvir and Yojano were returning, he pulled out a second smaller object, which was also wrapped in white cloth and again placed down on the table.

Stromvir sat down at a chair opposite Torano. A small but long wooden table sat between them. Yojano sat down next to his father, and his father began to speak.

"Stromvir, you must understand the importance of the journey we are asking you to depart on."

"Yes sir, I do. We must make contact with this new land for no other reason than to ensure peace between us." Stromvir replied confidently.

"You are correct. I trust you understand the dangers of the Endless Sea. In a few days' time, you will reach a point that has never been sailed on before, so even I cannot tell you what you may have awaiting you. I can, however, give you these." Torano said as he began unwrapping the first object. He carefully unwrapped the first object to reveal a large brass key. The key had ornate etchings in the metal and seemed to be extremely old. Handling it as though it was very delicate, Torano offered it to Stromvir.

"Use this only if needed, if the time comes, you will know." Torano said as he handed the key to Stromvir and carefully began unwrapping the second object. The second object was much smaller, and its purpose was unclear upon looking at it.

"I will say this, I have never used this before, so I cannot, with any certainty, tell you what it does. This is a whistle, a whistle I was told would help even in the gravest of situations, fortunately for me, I was never in such a situation. I was told that I would pass this down to the person who needed it most, and I believe that to be you." Torano explained as he handed Stromvir the small silver whistle. Upon inspecting it, Stromvir noticed there was some sort of bird-like figure etched into the face of the whistle. It was much heavier than it appeared. There was a small loop on one end where a string used to be, Stromvir pulled out some of the fishing line he always carried on him and made a necklace out of it. He put the necklace over his head and tucked the whistle inside his clothing.

"Thank you, sir. It is my hope I shall not have to use these, but I am glad that I have them." Said Stromvir graciously.

"You should find Jarena, you must be off soon" said Torano as he stood up from the table and motioned everyone outside.

"I would like a word with Stromvir, father., if you would not mind." Said Yojano.

"I shall wait outside."

Yojano paced the room for a minute, thinking of exactly what he wanted to say. Stromvir waited patiently for the emperor to speak, knowing there was importance in his coming words. After a moment that felt like an hour, Yojano finally spoke up.

"Stromvir, I want you to understand that you are doing Gremela a service that can never be repaid." He said. "When you arrive at the new land, I want you to send me a pixie, but not just any pixie, I want you to summon this one." He said as he snapped his fingers and a pixie appeared out of thin air. "This pixie will be able to deliver a message to me no matter where you are in the world."

Stromvir admired the pixie Yojano summoned, it was different from the rest. Most pixies were small and blue with green eyes, but this one was green with blue eyes, and seemed slightly larger than the others.

"I promised you upon your return you will have a place inside the castle on the sea and I stand by that promise, but there is more to it. I believe being my advisor would be a more suitable role for you." Yojano continued.

"Sir, I don't know what to say" Stromvir stammered.

"Please, call me Yojano, you have earned that much" Yojano said with a smile. "Now, you had better get going, it is almost Mid Day.

The two of them emerged from the hull of the ship and met with Jarena and Torano before going their separate ways.

"Are the two of you ready?" he asked.

"We are." They said in unison.

Stromvir was starting to get behind the helm when Yojano tapped him on the shoulder, looked him in the eye and said:

"Remember what I told you."

Stromvir looked back at him, flashed a half smile, and shook Yojano and Torano's hands. Yojano and his father scaled down the ship and into the rowboat below. Waving at the two captains as they embark on what would likely be the ship's last journey.

Aboard the Mare Domitor the entire crew comprised almost entirely of sentient wooden statues were ready and waiting for their command. Stromvir made his way onto the Captains Deck and stood at the edge of the ship looking out to the sea. He turned around to face his crew, his hands tucked neatly behind his back, and he gave the first command:

"Onward"

Just then, everyone on board the ship began to man their positions, the sails unrolled and were pulled tight, the weights were lifted from the sides of the ship, and the rudder was released. A large gust of wind seemingly came from nowhere to lunge the ship forward out toward the sea, away from the safety and comfort of the land they left behind. Stromvir stood behind the wheel of the ship, with Jarena next to him. The cool sea breeze was hitting his face and softly blowing his hair, and for the first time since this journey started, he felt a great sense of peace and hopefulness. Maybe the journey ahead would not be as hard as he imagined.

CHAPTER 6

THE CAVE

Life on the Sea was not always hard, but not always easy either. Several weeks had gone by since they left Gremela, the sea was in an extended state of calmness, which Stromvir knew could not last much longer. He had been preparing for the days when the sea would betray him and make the journey even more challenging.

Nearly every day for a week at night the skies would grow ominously dark, and cloudy, not a star in sight. This made it hard for even trained sailors such as Stromvir to navigate during the night. He had to rely on a small compass he had, to try to ensure he stayed on some sort of bearing. The ship was nearing the edge of where the sea had been charted, in just two days' time, they would be sailing on an uncharted sea, whose waters were unpredictable and were said to have a mind of their own. Stories from past journeys had depicted the water creating swells of nearly one hundred feet in a matter of minutes, with nearly no warning. Other stories told of how most of the journeys resulted in the disappearance of the ship and crew, never to be heard from again.

Stromvir was standing on deck behind the helm of the ship, admiring the view he was getting from the sunset when he suddenly realized there were no clouds in sight. Up until this night, thick clouds began to form overhead just before the sun began to set every night. Stromvir let the crew know and before long, the entire crew was standing on deck, looking up at the sky in admiration. It had been weeks since any of them had seen a sunset, or the stars.

The crew was on the deck nearly the entire night, sacrificing sleep for one night of stargazing seemed an easy choice to make on this night. They were all laying on their backs looking straight up at the sky, seemingly unbothered by the harsh waters they knew were coming. They were thankful for such a calm start to the journey. They savored every moment of the cloudless star filled night, making sure to enjoy every star they could see. Nearly everyone fell asleep on the deck of the ship that night, Stromvir and Jarena were no exception.

Stromvir awoke with a jolt and sat straight up, he looked to his side and Jarena was not present as she was when he had fallen asleep. He stood up and quickly realized he was alone on the ship, but also saw he was just offshore of an island he had never seen before. He could see that the life boats the ship was equipped with were at the shore, so to get to this island he would need to swim.

He dove into the water without hesitation and quickly swam ashore. When he got to shore, he could not find anyone, aside from a few pieces of clothing and some shoes the island seemed to be totally deserted. He walked further inland and began to realize he had made it to the island he was trying to find. He never thought it would happen this quick or this easy. The others must have let him sleep on the ship while they explored the island. He just needed to find them. He walked down the beach until he found a path that led into the woods. He followed the path deep into the woods, the underbrush and vegetation were so thick his progress was painfully slow. He had nothing on him to help, he had left his sword on the ship, and the island seemed to have nothing on it, there were no signs of humans anywhere. The trees he saw in this place were unlike anything he had ever seen before. The trees all had four trunks that were twisted around each other upward where they converged into one trunk that then branched into hundreds, if not thousands of smaller branches, the leaves were bright red on one side and yellow on the other. Upon resting his hand upon one of them he learned they were very rough textured, resting your hand on one of them for longer than a few seconds was almost painful.

He continued following the path until he came to the edge of a cliff. He had an excellent view of the island and for the first time, was able to judge the size of it. He looked out onto the horizon in front of him, from atop a mountain he had not realized he scaled, and below he saw more of the same trees that were surrounding him. The island was incredibly large, stretching out as far as he could see. The trees were everywhere and down below he could see they formed a path leading into the side of the mountain. He began looking for his path down when he realized there was not one. He would have to climb down the side of the cliff, it was not too high, but high enough for a fall from there to be fatal. Stromvir began scaling his way down the mountain and he made it to around twenty-five feet up when the branch he was holding onto snapped like a dead twig, and he lost his balance and plummeted down the rest of the way.

He landed with a blood curdling scream that no one could hear, he landed with all his weight on his ankle and snapped it. The crack was deafening, like a giant branch from a dead tree snapping off. He was immobilized, the pain was excruciating, he could go no further. He began the exceedingly painful task of dragging himself to the edge of the cliff, so he could prop himself up and have a proper look at his ankle. He was no more than a few feet from the side of the cliff, but every movement sent shockwaves of pain through his body, the pain was almost unbearable.

After nearly ten unbearably painful minutes, he had managed to drag himself to the cliff and prop himself up. There were a few plants and perhaps a stone or two within arm's reach, but nothing was readily available, he would have to crawl where he needed to go to collect supplies, he was going to attempt to fix his ankle as best he could.

Stromvir took a second to look at his ankle, the break was terrible, he could tell his bone was shattered inside of him. He needed to act fast if he wanted to avoid infection. He sat himself up once more and leaned his head against the hard stone wall. He sat like that for only a moment and when he opened his eyes, he noticed a figure in the distance. His vision was a little blurry so he could not quite make out what it was, but he could tell it was getting closer. He saw it leap and soar through the air and he knew it was a bird of some sort, it landed on a downed tree about fifty feet away and although it was much closer than before, it was still too far away for

Stromvir to see. He shut his eyes tight and gave them a second and opened them once more, his eyes were focused now but it seemed the creature had gone. He lowered his head in defeat, when he suddenly felt a presence just a few feet away. He was terrified to open his eyes, this was an unfamiliar island, this creature could be anything. He realized at that moment that he was not certain this creature was even friendly.

He opened his eyes to acknowledge the great creature, and to his surprise he saw a beautiful phoenix standing before him. The magnificent bird was staring down at him with blue marble-like eyes and a bright orange and red crest of feathers on the top of his head. Stromvir was frozen, staring back at the bird with admiration. Stromvir had never truly believed phoenixes existed until this moment.

The Phoenix came closer to Stromvir and bowed its head to him. Stromvir reached out his hand and pet the bird on the top of its head. The phoenix really seemed to enjoy this, and encouraged Stromvir to do it more by chasing his hand whenever he would pull it away. Stromvir laughed at this and for a second had forgotten about the amount of pain he had been in. The phoenix turned its head back down towards Stromvir's foot as if to examine his injury. The bird let out a deafening, but beautifully melodic call that immediately seemed to sedate the entire island even further. It began raining suddenly but it was no ordinary rain, the droplets were much larger, and they seemed to be mending Stromvir's ankle. Just a few minutes later, it seemed his foot had completely healed, he began to question his own sanity at that moment.

"Could this be real?" he thought to himself.

A moment later he was able to stand and walk again. His ankle was still in pain, but not nearly as much as before, it was a tolerable pain. He continued forward down the path ahead of him, until he reached the cliffside, which had an entrance to a cave at the base of it. Stromvir went inside the cave, and it was dark, so dark he could not see his hand in front of his face. He was only able to take a few steps at a time. The longer he stared into the vast darkness, he realized he was starting to make out faint outlines of things directly in front of him and before long he made his way to an opening in the cave, and there was a burning fire in the middle of it.

Stromvir quickly investigated the area and found an unused torch thrown on the ground near the fire. The fire was roaring but seemed to have no wood or other fuel keeping it ablaze. He quickly grabbed the torch and lit it so he could continue forward down the passage of the cave.

He thought he heard something from above him, like something was following him, but it was too dark to see more than a few feet above him. He made his way down the passage when he started to hear a faint noise, like a whisper. He continued toward the sound and eventually he realized it was a woman moaning, a painful, teary moan. He was now racing to find the woman, he fought his way through the darkness until he came to another opening. The room was vast, dark, and cold. The only light he could see was at the other end, where he saw a faint shadow, most likely the woman he heard. He noticed there was something on the ground up ahead, covering up most of the ground between him and the woman, who he could see was dressed in white, and was propped up against the wall, just as he had been a little while ago. He started walking toward her, and as he got nearer, he realized the floor was littered with the remains of his crew, all seemingly uninjured, but lifeless as they once were aboard the ship.

The helplessness and guilt had overcome him, but he pressed on toward the woman. He pushed his way through the darkness, refusing to look down at his feet. He made it to the woman, whose face was covered with her hair, and as he parted it to see her face, he fell backwards in shock. It was Jarena, she was clutching a large wound in her abdomen, blood was pouring from it as she was clutching it, and she was clearly struggling to breathe. Stromvir knew there was nothing he could do, so he grabbed her in his arms, sobbing and clutching her tightly. She was getting ready to speak when he suddenly heard the deafening call the phoenix made earlier, he looked up to see the phoenix perched high up in cave, then it flew out of sight. Once again it began raining, but yet again it was an even different rain, Stromvir was sitting with his face looking down at Jarena, but he felt the rain hitting his face as if he were lying on his back. The rain got heavier and heavier, attempting to fight it was no use. He laid his head back and when he raised it back up, he was back on the ship, in the exact place he was the night everyone was stargazing.

The entire experience had been a dream. He was thankful for such as it meant his wife was still alive and looking down to his side confirmed that. She was lying there, blissfully asleep, and unaware of the nightmare he had just experienced. Stromvir was relieved to see her and his crew back on the ship. It was just a dream, but it was too real. Stromvir could not shake the feeling that it was more than just a dream. Only time would tell. Stromvir looked up at the night sky for a moment longer before drifting back to sleep.

CHAPTER 7

THE FOREST

Yojano and his father stood at the edge of the beach watching the ship drift further and further out to sea and eventually out of sight. It slipped over the horizon just as the sun was setting, almost as if the sun pulled the ship down with it. He stood next to his father for what seemed like hours just staring out at the sea. He wondered if he had made the right decision, and wondered if he would ever see any of them again. He had grown fond of them over the last few days and was sad to see them go.

The next morning Yojano awoke before his father and went for a walk along the beach. He found a nice place to rest and clear his mind before they planned their next move. He knew his father wanted to go into the Continiata Forest in search of what attacked Reo and Kol. He could not shake the feeling that his father was hiding something from him, but he believed he would find out in due time.

He walked back to where he and his father camped for the night and found his father awake and preparing a breakfast of Loxie with some fresh potatoes and Gargon root. Yojano was none too fond of the Gargan Root, it looked like an oversize slimy slug, and tasted about the same. However, he knew Gargon root was full of nutrients, something he was sure to need if they were to journey into the forest.

"Ugh, Gargon Root, are you trying to kill me?" Yojano asked with a disgusted look on his face.

Torano gave a quick chuckle before serving Yojano the bigger of the two pieces of Gargon root.

"Better you than me" he replied with an even bigger chuckle.

After breakfast Torano confirmed Yojano's suspicions and said they needed to go to the forest.

"May I ask why we are still going? Reo and Kol made it back alive. We were going to look for them, now we needn't." Protested Yojano.

"We are going to find what they spoke of. We need to know what it is." Replied Torano seriously.

Yojano knew his father was not bluffing, and simply could not stand the thought of letting his father go there alone. He stood next to him, looking out at the sea, watching the waves crash against the tall rocks. He turned to see his father had already begun to walk away from the beach and towards the horses. Yojano reluctantly followed behind and when they reached the top of a hill, his father turned around and looked back at him, gave him a half-smile and continued on.

After reaching the horses, they continued east toward Keftingrav, a day's ride past the border and they will have reached the forest. It was more than a four-day ride there, they rode out of the gulley they were in and came to a clearing filled with Whistling Thistle and Morwood Chutes. They rode through the clearing and followed the well-worn road with the sun at their backs until they reached a place to camp for the night.

Yojano was hardly sleeping, instead his nights consisted of lying awake looking at the stars whilst his mind was filled with never ending anxiousness about the days to come. He knew he needed to be strong for his people, the people he was appointed to lead. He often thought of how he could lead if he was such a mess himself?

One particularly sleepless night, the third night out, was the worst for him. Just before sunset, a thin veil of dark clouds filled the sky, hiding the stars and making the night that much darker. A vast storm was heading straight for them, the biggest one Gremela had seen in years by the looks of the clouds. They were less than two days from the forest now, Yojano hoped they would make it there by the onset of the storm.

The next day the skies grew far darker than the day before, making Mid-Day seem as dark as night. The storm would be raging by the next day, Yojano could feel the crisp cool wind hitting his face with increasing force by the hour it seemed. Yojano usually preferred to sleep outside in a makeshift hammock, but he played the ear of caution that night and slept in the burlap tent he and his father had with them. The storms in Gremela were fierce and unpredictable, getting caught in one while sleeping would be far from pleasant.

Yojano and his father set off very early the next morning, it had not begun to rain quite yet, so they took advantage of this and continued making their way to the forest, they would be there within the hour if they made haste. The horses were trotting at a considerable pace as they came over a small hill and could see the forest at the bottom. They continued down the hill to the edge of the forest and found a good place to hitch their horses. The forest got thicker the farther you went, making navigating through it with a horse nearly impossible.

"What are we looking for in here father?" asked Yojano.

"You shall see soon enough."

Yojano was unsatisfied with this answer, but decided not to press it, whatever it is, it must be important. They pressed on into the forest, swords drawn and minds alert, the Continiata forest was filled with dangers both known and unknown, so exercising caution was a must.

After traversing the increasingly difficult landscape of the forest for a few hours Yojano's father finally wished to stop for a rest. When they sat down Yojano could tell his father had seen better days, he was pale, clammy, and seemed to be slightly confused.

"Father, what are we looking for? I must know or I shall not continue. This is far too dangerous for us, we are not properly prepared." Said Yojano

"Son, I believe you are right, but I fear perhaps it is too late for me now.."

Just then, Torano raised his shaking finger and pointed at something behind Yojano. Yojano was paralyzed with fear, but slowly turned around to see a group of werewolves in the distance. They had not seen them yet, but it was inevitable they would.

Yojano reached into this pack and pulled out a canteen full of water and gave some to his father. He drank almost the entire canteen in one go. His condition improved significantly as he finished, the color returned to his face, and he was no longer clammy and more than capable of walking again. Once Torano was on his feet, they tucked behind a tree to come up with a plan for getting past the werewolves.

"Father, this is madness! We simply cannot continue! There are at least four of them, and two of us. We are not exceptionally trained in combat!" Protested Yojano.

Torano peeked around the tree to survey what was coming, the look in his eye worried Yojano.

"Son, let me go on alone. This does not concern you."

Torano looked defeated, as if he accepted his fate. He peaked around the tree once more and slowly came out from behind the tree, crouched and began walking slowly towards a large rock formation near the werewolves, he was climbing over a downed tree when the tree suddenly snapped, and his father fell a few feet quickly to the ground. The snap was deafening, and as Yojano panicked he saw that the werewolves had turned their attention to the noise and began making their way closer to them. Torano had managed to stay perfectly still at the base of the log he had just fallen from.

Yojano could not see his father but knew he was still there, and saw the werewolves inching closer to him, none the wiser to his location when suddenly there was a sound from behind Yojano. The werewolves' heads shot up toward the noise and they saw Yojano standing there alone and terrified. He was frozen in that moment, knowing what was about to happen. The werewolves were climbing over the log when Torano stood up and slashed at one of them with his sword before running off. The werewolves all let out a deafening roar before running on all four legs after him. It was only a matter of seconds before they reached him.

Yojano stood in shock as he knew what was going on just over the hill from where he was. He could not believe it; he was still paralyzed from the thought of it. He let the thought paralyze him for just a few seconds more, and then he leapt up and charged full speed at the werewolves. He was determined to save his father or die trying. He could not let these creatures kill his father in front of him. His will to live was far stronger than his fear of death. When he reached the werewolves, he drew his sword and leapt onto one of the werewolves' backs, he hit it over the head with the hilt of his sword, causing it to buck wildly, throwing Yojano off and onto the cold ground below. Yojano landed on his back, the wind was knocked out of him. After a short moment he gathered himself and looked up to see the werewolf staggering toward him. Yojano braced himself and pointed his sword straight up, and the werewolf tumbled and fell backward onto the sword, and became quite still. Merely a moment had passed before Yojano had realized what he had done, and the remaining werewolves took notice as well for there was a definite cry of outrage from the others.

Yojano knew it would be only a few seconds until the other werewolves reached him, only a few seconds until they would come to retrieve their dead companion's body, leaving his own exposed and vulnerable. He tried to throw the werewolf from him, but it was too heavy, he was trapped. Trapped and waiting for his demise, which would come at any second. Defeated, he closed his eyes, awaiting the inevitable. He could hear heavy panting, it was coming closer and suddenly, he felt a great weight lift from his chest. He opened his eyes to see what he feared most, three scruffy black werewolves staring down at him, each with a grin bigger than the last. He lifted his hands in front of his face, a feeble attempt to protect himself when there was a loud crack. This drew the werewolves' attention away from Yojano. No sooner than they looked up, one of them suddenly had an arrow through its head, and it fell to the ground with a thud. One of the two remaining werewolves ran into the woods while the other turned its attention to whatever was in the woods and began sprinting into the dense forest, in chase of whatever was out there, whatever had just saved Yojano's life.

Yojano got up and surveyed his surroundings for a minute before taking off in the direction he thought he came from. He continued through the forest until he came to a small gulley with a freshwater stream and a small cove in one of the hillsides with tree roots covering it. This was the perfect place to rest, Yojano hurried over to the stream and refilled his canteen and started to clear out the cove so he could make a fire.

Yojano gathered some small firewood and sparked a fire with a piece of rock and the tip of his sword. Sleeping was most likely unwise, he decided to keep watch all night, the werewolves were accustomed to the night, he was not. Halfway through the night he was drifting in and out of sleep, the fire had died down just enough to be concealed within the cove, but still warm enough to stave off any coldness. It was quite cozy in the cove, as he began drifting to sleep, he thought he heard footsteps just downstream. He peeked his head out of the cove and much to his surprise, there was nothing there. As he was drifting off again, he heard them, only closer. Fully alert now he once again peeked his head out to see who was there and once again, there was no one. He figured his mind was playing tricks on him due to sleep deprivation and decided to sleep for a few hours if he could, after all, it was only a couple of hours until dawn.

When dawn broke Yojano was awoken by the sound of rustling close by, he quickly gathered his belongings and set off West, opposite the sun. He knew if he headed straight west for long enough, he would make it out of the woods.

He traveled for almost an hour when he was stopped in his tracks. In front of him, no more than fifty paces away, were more werewolves. They had yet to see him, so he immediately ducked behind a nearby Gargon tree. He was clutching his sword when he realized that there were more werewolves behind him, he was in between two groups.

He hardly had any other option but to sneak past the ones in front of him, the ones blocking his way out of the forest. He clutched his sword once more and slowly made his way through the trees, crawling under downed limbs and heavy brush whenever he could. He only had one shot at this, they were leisurely eating some sort of animal they had just caught so he had no need to distract them. He managed to sneak past them and was slowly making his way towards the edge of the forest, he could see it in the distance.

He was climbing down from a small outcropping of rocks when one of them shifted, causing the rest of them to tumble down the small hill they were situated on, this caught the attention of the werewolves, who would soon be upon him if he stayed. He took off in a full sprint toward the edge of the forest just after the werewolves had spotted him. He knew within seconds one of them would be upon him. He turned to see one leaping at him, he braced himself and pulled out his sword and thrust it toward the werewolf. He was tackled to the ground and was stuck under this werewolf when he realized his sword was gone. He struggled to work his way out from under the giant beast but it was too heavy once again. He saw only one other werewolf coming toward him when a small arrow went flying, impaling the other werewolf through the heart. It fell to the ground with a horrible thud.

A man with elegant robes and a crossbow came from somewhere out of view and retrieved his arrow before turning around and running toward Yojano.

Yojano watched as this man made his way over to him and extended his hand.

"I am trapped under here, perhaps help me push this beast off?" Yojano asked graciously.

"Of course, your Majesty" replied the man.

They struggled for a while to push the great beast off Yojano, but eventually they succeeded. They walked a short distance to the edge of the forest where Yojano immediately collapsed to the ground in pure bliss. He wept for several minutes before he was able to gather himself.

"Thank you for that, I owe you my life" said Yojano as he bowed to this man.

"Your majesty, it is an honor. I would do it thrice over given the chance."

"I stand by what I said, now do tell me, what is your name?" asked Yojano.

"Aurendel" he replied.

"Well, Aurendel, please do accompany me back to the castle. I've seen enough of this forest for a lifetime."

Aurendel and Yojano walked back to Aurendel's house which was situated atop a small hill just west of the tree line. He had a perfect view of the forest on one side, and the other side had a beautiful view of a wide-open grassland as far as one could see. The place was small, but comfortable enough for one person to enjoy. After Aurendel gathered the things he needed, they headed off to the Castle on the Sea.

They awoke at first light the next morning and began taking down the campsite. Gathering up the burlap tent and the sleeping rolls, and of course putting the fire out. Aurendel piled several large boughs of pine needles on the fire before they set off. The trail was unusually quiet this early in the morning. It was easier to hear oneself think at times like these.

"Aurendel, do tell me, how did you know where I was?" asked Yojano, the question had been burning in him since the previous day.

"Well, that's easy, I was following you of course." He said.

"You were, what?" asked Yojano, a puzzled look on his face.

"Well, I saw you and your father go in, and I didn't see you come out. I went in just before the sun was setting. That's when I heard the first howl." Aurendel said. "I followed the sound and before long I could see you just over the hill. I could see you were in trouble."

"Well, I am glad you were there Aurendel. I really do owe you my life."

They trotted on in silence for a while longer, enjoying the fresh breeze in their faces, and the smell of burning cedar coming from a small hut in the distance.

"You seem to know the forest quite well" said Yojano.

"I do." Replied Aurendel. "I hunt most of my food in there. I never go too deep though, there's no telling what could be in there."

These words pierced Yojano like a hot knife. How could his father have sent them in there? That was the most dangerous place he had ever been in. He began to wonder if things would be different had he protested. Told his father it was simply foolish to go in there. His father, and he shuddered to think of it, might still be alive.

"I can never repay the debt I owe you, Aurendel. You seem like a capable man. A man who can handle himself. If you would, please join me as my Chief Counsel."

"My word, sir. I do not know what to say" Aurendel replied.

"I shall take that as a yes. We will be arriving soon."

They had the warmest of welcomes upon their arrival back at the castle, but many of those at the castle also seemed concerned about the absence of Torano. This was a question that was promptly addressed by Yojano.

"Torano, my Father, has gone. I do not wish to speak of this any further at the present."

This stifled questions for the time being, but Yojano knew it was only a matter of time before he must face these questions. A few days seemed more than enough time to come up with something to say.

"Who is this, sir?" called out a voice from within the small crowd of people, pointing at Aurendel.

"This is Aurendel, my new Chief Counsel" replied Yojano.

The crowd dispersed suddenly, and everyone went back to what they were doing. Aurendel followed Yojano as they walked through the castle. They came to a stop at a large room with an oversized bed and a window with a view of the sea. The room was equipped with everything a person could need, a wardrobe, bookshelves, an oil lamp, a wash basin.

"These are your quarters, Aurendel. Please make yourself at home."

CHAPTER 8

THE RAGING SEAS

The sky was a soft shade of pink and orange when Stromvir awoke at sunrise. The Sea was calm, at least for the moment. He woke up to discover Jarena had already awoken and was somewhere within the ship. Stromvir did not know how to tell her about the dream he had, he figured it was best to keep it to himself.

The ship was at full sail, and they were making great progress through the endless sea. Stromvir stood up and made his way to the bow of the ship to survey what was ahead. He pulled out his compass to ensure they were still on the same bearing they had been on since they left. They were at a part of the sea that was too calm, and too empty, it seemed almost unreal. There was nothing in every direction, just water and clouds. When Stromvir awoke, the clouds were almost non-existent, but within just a couple of hours, the sky grew ominously dark with storm clouds once again, and the crew of the ship prepared for a massive storm that was looming overhead.

At this point, they had spent more days encumbered by a massive storm than they spent in clear skies, everyone had grown accustomed to being cold, wet, and slightly miserable. The constant storming was diminishing what was left of the crew's morale.

"Ay' Captain! What are we doing out here? There's nothing out here!" said one of the crew members.

"I know, but there will be, and we must be ready when we find it." Stromvir replied with a wink and a pat on the shoulder.

The crewman seemed unsatisfied with this answer as he gave a low grumble and went below deck to his plinth where he stayed the rest of the afternoon. For a moment the next morning, the rain ceased, and the sun showed itself between a small break in the rain clouds. This improved the visibility of what was ahead. Stromvir once again walked down to the bow of the ship, trying to see if there was anything in the distance while he could.

As he was looking out to sea, he noticed something in the distance, he could not see where the water ended, and the sky began. There was a moment of confusion before the realization hit him. They were heading directly for a massive wave, well over one hundred feet tall.

Stromvir ran back up to the deck where the helm sat and rang the bell to alert everyone to man their positions. When everyone was on deck, he showed them what he was looking at, and one of the members handed him a spyglass to get a better view. He was indeed correct in what he had seen, it was a wave like he had never seen before, and they would be there within just a few minutes at the speed they were traveling.

Stromvir hurried inside to find Jarena, who was still somewhere inside the hull of the ship. He went down to their quarters and she was sitting on the edge of their bed with tears in her eyes. Stromvir knew what was wrong without asking, he knelt next to her.

"Jareth is okay, Jarena. He is much safer there than he is here, especially right now."

Before he could finish, she looked up at him, knowing something was wrong. He stood up and offered his hand. She took his hand, and they ran up on deck together. Upon arriving on deck, Jarena laid her eyes on the colossal wave that was before them and her heart began to race, her chest felt heavy. She and Stromvir had taken on big waves before but never quite this big.

Everyone was frantically running around the ship, trying to man their position before it was too late.

Stromvir was shouting out commands as well as Jarena. They were prepping the ship to turn hard to starboard, positioning the ship parallel to the wave. Everyone was in their positions and as they began turning the ship, the wave suddenly dissipated, and for a little longer than a few seconds it was completely calm, and then suddenly, the wave had turned from one large wave to hundreds of smaller waves, they were caught in a tsunami, facing sideways to the current, and the waves were tossing the ship in every direction, it was impossible to turn or maneuver the ship at all.

"BRACE YOURSELVES" Stromvir bellowed to the crew. Everyone grabbed ahold of something and held on for their lives. Stromvir was trying to get up, he thought if he could just reach the helm, they may have a chance. He was waiting for the right moment to stand up and as he found it, he stood up and jumped for the helm. He landed just in front of it and was able to grab ahold just before a wave sent the ship sideways toward an oncoming wave. He stood up and began to right the ship as much as he could when he saw they were headed straight for a massive swell, there was no avoiding it. They were floating up the swell and when they reached the peak there was a short moment where everything felt almost weightless. Stromvir peered over the side of the ship and saw that once again, the colossal wave was back, and they were on top of it. They were more than one hundred feet in the air, and at any moment would begin plummeting down to the surface.

The ship's nose pointed down and the ship was racing toward the surface, with no conceivable way of stopping or slowing down, much of any motion at this speed would rip the ship apart. He had an idea, and he only had one chance at it. He gripped firmly onto the helm and waited for the perfect moment.

They were hurdling towards the surface at incredible speed, and when they got close enough, Stromvir spun the helm hard to starboard, with the speed they were going the force of this caused the ship to list to starboard, so much so the ships giant masts were caught in the wave, causing them to slow down and land on the keel of the ship.

They made it. Stromvir gathered himself for a moment before addressing the crew. There were suddenly three loud cracks, Stromvir and the crew looked up and saw the two topsails and the main mast crashing down on them. Everyone ducked out of the way as the pieces of the mast narrowly missed the main deck of the ship, only hitting small sections on the sides, causing minimal damage.

Stromvir knew this was going to be more difficult now with the damage to the sails. He pulled his crew together and encouraged them to be hopeful, and ensured them they could continue, albeit slower than before.

The next morning Stromvir awoke to a peaceful pink and orange sunrise that could illuminate even the darkest of rooms. He went out on the main deck and was greeted by one of the wooden crew members.

"Aya' Sir, my name is Jarven. I have something to show you." He said "I was on watch last night up in the crow's nest and I noticed something."

He pulled out his compass and the needle was spinning out of control. Stromvir gave a concerned look as he pulled out his compass to find the same thing was happening.

"Thank you for bringing this to my attention, Jarven" said Stromvir as he continued inspecting his compass. He went to the bow of the ship to see if there was anything on the horizon.

His eyes widened and he nearly dropped his compass:

"Jarven!" shouted Stromvir from the bow of the ship.

"Yes sir!" he said breathlessly as he ran over to Stromvir.

"Please go and fetch me a spyglass, quickly!"

Jarven ran off and came back a few moments later holding a spyglass and handed it to Stromvir. He fully extended it and held it up to his eye. In the far distance, almost too far for even the spyglass to see, he saw land. His heart was full of relief and joy at this moment, he handed the spyglass to Jarven and motioned for him to look.

"My word! You have done it sir! You found it!" said Jarven in excitement.

"*We* found it, but keep it down, Jarven! It might just be Gremela, we were thrown in every direction" replied Stromvir. "Let's keep this quiet until we figure out where we are."

Stromvir ordered the crew to continue at full speed, which was now significantly slower than before due to the damage to the ship's mast. Before long the land in the distance was visible even to the naked eye, though still quite far off. The crew was relieved and celebrating, they were running around wrapping their arms around each other and singing and dancing. Soon enough, as the island inched ever closer, Jarven took his spyglass and looked through it to see an island that was clearly not Gremela on the horizon. He pulled the spyglass down for a moment when something caught his eye nearby in the water.

Once again using his spyglass, he noticed the water turning a darker shade of blue just off in the distance.

"Captain! Over here!" he shouted to Stromvir.

Stromvir could see the cautious look in his eye, and quietly made his way over to him.

"Sir, you should see this" said Jarven as he handed Stromvir the spyglass once more.

Stromvir looked through the glass and saw what Jarven saw, but it was worse than he thought. As they got closer, he noticed there was a tear in the water, a giant gap stood between them and the island they sought. They were headed straight for the gap which seemed to be an endless dark abyss. If they could just make it across the gap, they could make it.

"My word Jarven, we must act now!" Stromvir shoved the spyglass back into Jarven's hands and ran off to the helm.

"Man your positions everyone, now!" bellowed Stromvir.

Everyone looked very confused for a moment before realizing he was serious and began to man their positions. Stromvir shouted out an order for a hard to port steer, they were going to turn the ship around to think of a plan.

He gripped the helm and spun it hard to port and the ship slowly began to turn, and they were slowly inching closer to the abyss below. The damage made the ship turn unbearably slow.

The ship was halfway turned around and now parallel with the edge of the water, mere inches from the abyss. The ship was not moving, they were stranded. They were floating in the same spot for several minutes when suddenly the ship jerked and threw everyone to the ground, including Stromvir. He stood up and saw the water was slowly starting to move toward the abyss, pushing them slowly along. There was no time, they would be sent over the edge in no more than a minute. Stromvir fell to his knees in a moment of desperation, causing the necklace he wore to fall out from underneath his shirt.

He looked down and saw the whistle Torano had given him before he left. He remembered what Torano had told him:

"Even in the gravest of situations"

He could not think of any situation that could be graver, so without thinking he pulled off the cap of the whistle and blew into it. Nothing happened, no sound emitted from it. He ripped the necklace off in frustration and threw it to the ground, once more fell to his knees and began pounding on the ground with his fists. Jarven was standing on the bow of the ship, watching it inch closer to the abyss when suddenly the most beautiful song he had ever heard emitted from the sky. It grew louder with every passing second. This caught the attention of everyone on board, including Stromvir.

There was suddenly a strong gust of wind that pushed them away from the edge, but only just. A great winged figure came out from above the clouds, singing louder than before. It came closer to them and Stromvir could see it was the Phoenix he had seen in his dream. The Phoenix kept calling and before long two more had joined him. The abyss was filling in and the water was crashing against the ship violently causing the ship to list right and left quickly. The force of this caused what was left of the masts to snap, rendering the ship motionless.

The Phoenix's gave one last call before flying off toward the island, as if they lived there. The ship was still, the water was calm. Stromvir stood behind the helm, looking into the distance. He had no idea how to continue, there were no sails. If he sent the crew down to the cargo hold to row, it would take days of nonstop rowing to get there, and everyone, although most of the crew was made of wood, was exhausted.

Jarena had joined Stromvir behind the helm and put her hand on his shoulder. They stood there for a few minutes enjoying the silence before Stromvir spoke.

"We did it, but we are not there yet." Stromvir said with a hint of frustration in his voice. They were still several miles offshore and had no conceivable way of getting there. Stromvir leaned his back against the helm, and his weight caused the helm to shift forward slightly.

He turned to face the helm and noticed the center had opened to reveal a keyhole. He pulled the wrapped-up brass key that Torano had given him earlier.

"It cannot be this easy, surely?" he asked himself as he stuck the key in the hole and turned it. At that moment, there was a deafening noise coming from below the deck. The great wooden gargoyles in the cargo hold came to life and sat down on the benches between the port holes of the ship. They extended their giant oars and fed them through the holes and submerged them in the water and began to row. The ship lunged forward and was moving at a considerable pace. Before long they were close enough to land to see there was a small cluster of creatures waiting on the beach for them.

Stromvir removed the key in hopes of stopping the gargoyles from rowing, but they persisted and before long, the ship had run aground along the shore and was permanently beached. The Mare Domitor had made its final voyage.

CHAPTER 9

CENTAURIA

Stromvir was the last to disembark the ship, watching over his crew, ensuring their safety after a long journey. There were three creatures of the like Stromvir had never seen before waiting patiently on the beach. They seemed to be a peaceful group, as Stromvir figured they would have attacked by now if they were going to. Stromvir led his wife and living crew members toward the mysterious creatures and was the first to speak as they reached them.

"Greetings, my name is Stromvir. We have come in peace from Gremela." He said calmly.

The three creatures shared a somber and cautious look at one another before the foremost one spoke.

"In peace? From *Gremela?*" he asked hesitantly.

"Yes, we were sent here by our emperor, Yojano, in search of a new land. We want to make peace." Replied Stromvir as he bowed to them.

"Yojano? Is he a descendant of Mercado?" asked the horse-like creature.

"Mercado? He has not held the throne in over 2000 years. Are you from his time?" asked a confused Stromvir.

"Not we, but our ancestors. Our kind were driven out of Gremela thousands of years ago, and with nowhere to go, our ancestors found this place. We have been living here in peace and exile ever since. We did what we could to hide this place, using a mixture of present and ancient magic. Our ancestors were fearful Mercado may come looking for them." Said the other horse-like creature.

"I do not wish to be indelicate, but what are you?" asked Stromvir.

The creature on the left was a horse-like creature with a long horn sticking out from the middle of its head, and its coat was white as snow, blindingly reflecting the sun. The creature was simply radiant and was indescribably the most beautiful thing any of them had ever seen.

"I am Octavia, the Unicorn" replied Octavia as she bowed to Stromvir and Jarena.

The creature in the middle resembled a horse as well, although he had horse legs, his torso and head were that of a man.

"I am Argosh, the Centaur" replied Argosh.

The third creature was so short Stromvir had almost forgotten he was there when he spoke up:

"I'm Resnik, the Gnome." Replied the gnome, who could not have been more than two feet tall.

"It is my honor to meet you all, I assure you, we mean you no harm." Said Stromvir reassuringly. "What do you call this place?"

"Centauria" replied Argosh.

"Apparently not everyone at the time was too fond of the name, and I wonder why.." said Octavia as she looked at Argosh with a curious look in her eyes.

"Ya, me ancestors did naw' like the name much, but you see we had not a choice in the matter you see" stammered Resnik. "We are but gnomes you see."

"Resnik, enough now. They have only just arrived, let's not bore them with the disagreements of our ancestors. Come now, we must head back. It is not far." Said Argosh as he motioned for the group to follow him.

Stromvir, Jarena and the rest of the crew followed them for a little more than an hour through a valley covered in towering trees and teeming with wildlife, most of which Stromvir had never seen before. Before long they reached an opening in the trees and were delighted to see a busy village, full of other Unicorns, Centaurs and Gnomes, all smiling and pleasantly greeting one another. One particular gnome tried to annoy Resnik by throwing a rock at him as he passed. He responded by aiming the staff he was wielding in his direction. The other gnome retreated into a small tent that looked big enough only for a dog while muttering something under his breath.

"Annoying 'ittle pig he is, idnt' he?" Resnik asked rhetorically.

Argosh led them into an immense tent at the top of a small hill that was overlooking the village. Stromvir had so many questions and was eager to ask them. At the far end of the tent sat three ornate chairs made of a shimmering stone, one for each of the leaders of Centauria. Octavia, Argosh, and Resnik took their respective seats and before Stromvir had a chance to speak Argosh spoke.

"You must have questions, I have answers. Please, let me know what answers you seek." Argosh said reassuringly.

"Now that Mercado is gone, can peace between Centauria and Gremela be achieved?" Stromvir asked.

"Certainly, but we must meet the new emperor first. Can you send for him?" asked Argosh.

"We can, but we haven't any means of contact, will a pixie work here?" asked Stromvir.

"Oh yes, we use them quite often, some even live here. Magical creatures tend to befriend other magical creatures. I must warn you though, the Gremela you left is no more. Traveling here costs one a great many things, and one of them is time. Please, show me your hand" Argosh requested.

Stromvir stuck out his hand and Argosh stared into it, mumbling some sort of incantation when suddenly, a plume of black smoke rose from his hand and swirled around. Stromvir could tell that the three leaders could see something in the smoke, and their faces became grimmer every second.

"I have seen everything that has happened since you left" said Argosh excitedly.

Jarena shoved Stromvir aside and was frantically looking at the smoke, trying to see what they saw, but could not.

Argosh closed his eyes once more and muttered a short incantation. Suddenly, Stromvir and Jarena could see an adult man standing in the middle of a small island, talking to a group of people who were encircling him, the scene shifted and suddenly they could see the same man, rescuing a much older looking Yojano from a man with long red hair.

Jarena broke into an uncontrollable fit of hysterics as she realized what she had seen. Stromvir was still puzzled, he turned to Argosh.

"Just how long has it been since we left? asked Stromvir.

Octavia, Argosh, and Resnik all exchanged a few concerned looks at one another.

"Well, this is beyond anything we imagined. It's been... twenty-seven years. Your son Jareth, was chosen to become the Solistima, and played a critical role in saving Gremela from another awful tyrant like Mercado."

Argosh replied solemnly. Jarena began to weep uncontrollably. How was it they traveled through time like they had?

"Twenty-seven years?!" Exclaimed Stromvir! "How can this be possible?! My son is almost the same age as me now!" He simply could not bring himself to believe they had traveled twenty-seven years through time. Jarena was in a fit of despair, Stromvir collapsing at her side to provide comfort, pointless though it was. They sat in tears for a while longer before remembering what they were here for. Stromvir stood up first, extending his hand out to Jarena. They both stood and turned to Argosh.

"Our ancestors experienced a time jump as well, although, there is no way to be sure how large theirs was." Argosh explained. "It is an unfortunate consequence of traveling on the endless sea and only those who have sailed it and lived to tell the tale know about it. It is likely that your leader did not know this would happen." Argosh explained, providing a small amount of reassurance. It was at least a little comforting to know that Yojano had not sent them here knowing what would happen. Stromvir knew there was nothing more to do, and nothing more to be said. There was no changing what happened. He turned to Argosh and spoke.

"So, the Solistima? He has returned?" asked Stromvir with a shocked expression.

"Yes. Jareth is he."

Stromvir turned around and paced around the room for a minute, Jarena next to him, and before long he knew what he had to do. He called for a pixie, scribbled the symbol of The Mare Domitor on a spare piece of parchment, and when the pixie arrived, he told it to find Yojano at the Castle on the Sea and deliver the message.

The pixie delivered the message only a few moments later, but it was the twenty-seven-year older Yojano who received the message.

"I trust you all need a bit of rest, please follow Resnik here to your new quarters. You are welcome in Centauria. Please do not make me regret that decision." Said Argosh as he motioned for Resnik to show them the way.

Resnik the gnome was short and stubby; a big belly was almost busting out of the green tunic he was wearing. His beet red face could hardly be seen behind his long mane of bushy red hair and scraggly beard. He was slightly smaller than the other gnomes as far as Stromvir could tell. Resnik led them down a long corridor with seemingly endless doors on either side. When they got to the end of the corridor there was a door on either side of them. Stromvir and Jarena took the room on the right, and Reo and his brother Kol took the room on the left.

The room was immense and unlike anything Stromvir or Jarena had ever laid eyes on before. It was a large circular room with a giant tree emerging from the ground in the center of it. The walls were covered in vines with beautiful purple flowers on them.

"Get some rest, will yas'? Time'll catch uptya' you see" Resnik said as he shut the door behind him and walked slowly back down the corridor.

Night had fallen when Jarena and Stromvir decided to sleep. Their journey had been terribly exhausting, and it was nice to be back on solid ground. Stromvir lay awake most of the night, thinking all the time of his son, who was now the Solistima. He wanted to see him, to hug him, tell him how proud he was. The thoughts of what could be and will be flooded his mind, he tried everything he could to shake them, but it was no use. He wondered if Yojano had received his pixie yet. He was hoping tomorrow he would wake up to his son and Yojano being there to greet him. The mere thought of that alone calmed his mind enough to allow him to drift off into sleep, putting his thoughts to sleep with him.

Stromvir awoke with a jolt the next morning. Something felt different, he felt different. He felt as if he had been stretched out and compressed multiple times throughout the night. His whole body was aching, as if he had fallen from a great height. His vision was coming and going, his hearing was failing him, and he could barely move himself to get out of bed. Jarena was still asleep beside him when suddenly she too sat up with a jolt and a shriek.

"Strom, I feel very strange." She said as she also attempted to get out of bed.

Stromvir was looking at Jarena and let out a loud gasp of horror. Her hair was turning from the usual dark brown to a lighter brown with grey and white patches all over. Her face was turning from silky smooth and radiant to a slightly worn and wrinkled face. Jarena also noticed these things about Stromvir. His hair, instead of being all black, was now mostly grey with subtle hints of black throughout. His thick beard was now mostly grey and was growing more and more with every second. Within just a few minutes, his hair, beard, and moustache had all grown to an uncontrollable length. He tripped on his beard when he was finally able to stand up.

As he was getting up the door to their room burst open. Reo and Kol stood in the doorway, and by the looks of them they were having the same problem.

"What is happening to us?" Reo demanded.

"I am unsure, Reo. I say we need to find Resnik, or Argosh."

Kol, being the only one who was able to walk at this point, ran to get the others. Stromvir, Jarena and Reo all sat on the floor in agonizing pain, wondering what was happening to them. Moments later Argosh rounded the corner with Resnik at his ankles.

"Hahahah, I told 'em this'd appen' didn' I?" Resnik said as he struggled to contain his laughter.

"You did Resnik, but, laughing will do them no good." Replied Argosh.

"What is happening to us?" Stromvir asked as he gave Resnik a less than happy look.

"Well, it seems time has already begun the process of catching up to you." Said Argosh calmly.

"It usually takes a bit longer to start, but at least it will be over within a day or so."

"What do you mean time is "catching up"? asked Stromvir.

"Well, you left Gremela twenty-seven years ago, but to you it was only a few weeks." Argosh explained. "Time is the one thing you cannot escape from or get back. Your body skipped ahead in time twenty-seven years, and now it must catch up."

Argosh could tell Stromvir and Jarena seemed thoroughly displeased with this answer. Knowing he was still unclear, he explained further.

"You are going through a process of rapid aging, your body is aging the years you were gone all at once, and it's quite painful I imagine. No matter, within a day, you should be back to normal again."

Stromvir, Jarena and Reo were standing there staring at Argosh as if he had just cut off his own arm. They could not believe what they were hearing.

"The best thing for you is rest. Please do rest some more. You shall be fine tomorrow. We have more to discuss, and quite a long walk ahead of us. You shall need your strength." Said Argosh as he left the room.

PART TWO

CHAPTER 10

THE FOREST ONCE MORE

<u>Present Day</u>

Yojano was standing on the moonlit terrace listening to the waves crash into the rocks below. Jareth and he were preparing for their journey to the new land the formers parents discovered. The discovery that Stromvir and Jarena were alive was both blissful and frightening. Had it taken them all this time just to arrive? How long had they been gone? So many questions were running through his mind, he decided it was time to get some sleep.

Yojano returned to his quarters and laid in bed for several hours before he was finally able to fall asleep. His sleep was far from enjoyable, being awoken every other hour from dreams and visions he was having of the sailors he sent away all those years ago. The knowledge that he sent them to their death took years to settle in, and it was a guilt that Yojano had been carrying all this time.

The idea that he may see them once more was unbelievable, and the number of possible outcomes of their reunion ran through his head. Yojano was unsure of how Stromvir and Jarena themselves felt about this, for the note said nothing, only the symbol of the Mare Domitor.

When morning arrived Yojano rose from his bed and went into the main dining hall. He sat in one of the mahogany chairs that were lined along either side of the grand mahogany table. There was a small porcelain tea set on the table in front of him. He grabbed two of the teacups from the set and filled them with a boiling hot green liquid. He placed the extra cup, now filled to the brim with the hot green liquid, at the chair directly to his right, and then proceeded to lean back in his own chair and take a drink of his own tea.

Moments later Jareth appeared in the dining hall, sat next to the emperor, and took a drink of his tea. He was repulsed by the drink, trying his best to not spit it out on the spot.

"Sir, what is this? Not to be unappreciative but it's quite dreadful." Asked Jareth, trying to hide the repulsion on his face.

"Gargon Root tea, I too find Gargon Root quite repulsive, but we need the strength." He replied with a slight chuckle.

"Sir, I think it's time you told me where we are going and what we are seeking." Said Jareth with a slight edge to his voice.

"I agree." Yojano replied.

He told Jareth the entire story of what happened after he was made emperor. He started with the day of his coronation and in painstaking detail, told Jareth everything that happened up until he was rescued from the forest by Aurendel. Tears had swelled up in his eyes when he was reciting the story of what happened to his father. He wished more than anything that he could tell his father they had succeeded, but he knew that was an impossibility. He continued and when he finished Jareth looked at him with both admiration and concern in his eyes. He looked down at his feet for a moment before looking back at the emperor.

"So, we are going to the forest to find what you and your father sought?" asked Jareth.

"I believe we must." Replied Yojano solemnly

"Well, when do we leave?" asked Jareth with a glint of excitement in his voice.

"Tomorrow, at first light." Responded Yojano as he took the last sip of his tea, wincing as it went down.

Yojano left the table to head for his quarters. Jareth too got up and went for his quarters, he needed to rest as much as anyone else. They both spent the day in their quarters, preparing for the journey to the forest. However, later that night Jareth found his mind a bit stretched, being pulled this way and that with the thoughts in his head. He had no recollection of his parents, when he was a kid he would sometimes have dreams about them. He spent a great deal of time wondering if the parents he saw in his dreams were really his parents at all, or merely a figment of his imagination.

There was a chance that within one week, he would be reunited with them after all this time. The thoughts in his head were dizzying, but he knew remaining calm was more important than ever.

The next morning, Jareth awoke and went out onto the terrace to look out at the sea for a while. When he arrived there was a perfect golden red hue peeking out from the horizon, illuminating the sky a soft pinkish orange, and the sea was glistening with the reflections of sun. Much to his surprise, Yojano was already out there as well, doing the very thing he was doing.

No more than a moment after Jareth arrived next to him, Yojano turned and looked at Jareth solemnly. He had been preparing for this moment since he sent them away all those years ago.

"Jareth, I have lived with the guilt of you growing up without your parents. I had just taken over for my father when he convinced me of the importance of their mission. I was a fool, I thought I had no choice, but I was mistaken. I hope one day, you can forgive me for what I have done." Yojano said to Jareth as tears began to swell in his eyes.

Jareth did not know what to say, he never blamed Yojano for what happened. It was a long time ago and people make mistakes.

"Sir, I do not blame you for what happened. You were only doing what you thought was right at the time. My parents also made a choice." He said to Yojano reassuringly.

"You are not angry with me? You have every right to be."

"Would being angry offer a sensible solution? I think not, besides, it just gets in the way." Replied Jareth.

"Gets in the way of what, may I ask?" asked Yojano rather genuinely.

"Moving on." Jareth said as he turned back towards the sea and gazed into its mesmerizing vastness. Their eyes were locked on the horizon for a long while before they both agreed it was time to be off. Yojano made all the necessary preparations with his wife and made sure everyone knew what to do in his absence.

"Jareth, wait here. I shall return momentarily." Said Yojano as he walked back into the castle.

Jareth stood on the edge of the terrace, preparing to cross the giant marble bridge which was now a permanent fixture of the landscape. Jareth waited a few moments before the emperor returned with Tullamore, who had been in jail no more than a few days but looked as if he were locked up years ago and forgotten. Perhaps his brief stint of imprisonment did him well.

"This fine gentleman here is going to accompany us on our journey to the forest. Are you not, Tullamore?" asked Yojano contemptuously.

"Yes…I am coming with, now unhand me you filthy animal" shrieked Tullamore.

"Animal? Quite funny coming from a cowardly traitor, now be quiet and move." Replied Yojano as he gave Tullamore a gentle shove in the right direction. They all crossed the bridge and at the other end there were three horses waiting for them. Yojano allowed Jareth to choose which horse he wanted first, then he selected his own, and instructed Tullamore to get on the remaining horse. He did so, and after he did Yojano attached a lead around Tullamore's waist and tied it off onto a loop in his saddle.

"Just in case you were thinking about running." Yojano said as he locked eyes with Tullamore and winked.

Jareth interjected

"Sir, we do not need to take horses" he said "I can have us there almost instantly. Have you forgotten?"

Yojano dismounted his horse, instructed Tullamore to do the same, and patted the horses on the back and they trotted off to their stable. Jareth instructed them to hold on to him. When he felt two hands grasp him, he clenched his hands together and took them with him into the compressing darkness. They were spinning out of control, their vision was stretching and there was a constant deafening hum in their ears. Just when Yojano and Tullamore thought they couldn't handle it anymore, their feet touched solid ground, their lungs expanded and took in more air than they ever had in their life, and they staggered as they stood up.

They took a few minutes to gather themselves, the sensation of traveling with Jareth was nauseating.

"I imagine it takes a bit of getting used to." Jareth said with a chuckle.

"Not sure how anyone could get used to *that.*" Tullamore stated.

No more than a few moments had passed when Yojano spoke up. He seemed concerned and scared about the coming journey. The look on his face was that of outright fear.

"Has either one of you been inside this forest before?" Yojano asked.

They both shook their heads, which was no surprise seeing as how neither one of them was from this side of Gremela. He continued.

"We must stick together in there, there are many inhabitants of the forest. Many of which we do not want anything to do with, but the most fearsome one we must deal with is the werewolves that dwell within. The forest is home to a great number of werewolves, we must remain vigilant." Yojano stated boldly.

Jareth and Tullamore looked uneasily at Yojano before nodding their heads in acknowledgement.

"I will lead the way" Yojano said as he began approaching the edge of the forest. All three of them entered the forest and it was dark immediately, the sun could not shine through the thickness of the trees. Jareth was concerned about the usefulness of his powers at present, he needed sunlight to be able to channel it. Just as the thought crossed his mind, the light in the center of the sun pendant flickered off. He tried to use some of his powers as a test, and nothing happened. He felt a sudden sense of panic as his combat skills were far from the best, but he knew that Yojano and Tullamore were well trained in combat.

They pressed on for hours and hours in the thick and unpierceable darkness until finally, they saw a flicker of majestic blue light in the distance. They all looked at each other and jeered in happiness and relief. They had no idea what the blue light was, but after hours of blinding darkness, any light was something to celebrate.

Painstakingly they continued on toward the light, stumbling over fallen limbs of the surrounding trees, Tullamore nearly slid down an embankment into what could only have been a fast flowing stream. After many near injuries and a lot more bickering amongst themselves, they reached the clearing the light resided in.

At first, it was hard to tell what the light was, but as they got nearer they determined it to be a magnificent fountain made of white stone. The base of the fountain was a large circle, filled to the brim with bright blue water. Floating in the water on one side of the fountain was a small basin of the same water. The water in the smaller basin was almost completely gone. In the center of the fountain stood a tall white spire, which contained two more smaller basins as it came to a point. The top of the fountain had six faces carved into it and was perpetually releasing the water into the topmost basin, which spilled over into the remaining basins. Jareth approached the base of the fountain and noticed a stone with writing etched in it had been placed on the edge of the fountain.

The three men approached the front most part of the fountain, trying to figure out how to activate it. The three of them all walked around the fountain, looking for any sort of switch or other mechanism that may activate the fountain. They were all standing close when suddenly, the lights on the fountain grew extraordinarily bright. A few moments later, a voice echoed through the woods.

"What brings you to my forest?" asked the mysterious voice.

"We seek answers" replied Yojano hesitantly.

"I have answers, but not without something in return," said the mysterious voice.

"What is it you require?" asked Yojano.

"One of you must drink from the fountain." said the voice.

Yojano remembered what happened when Kol drank from the water, it had driven him mad.

"And, if we refuse?" asked Yojano.

"Then I am afraid I cannot help you, traveler." Said the voice solemnly.

"I shall do it!" Tullamore volunteered. Before Yojano or Jareth had a chance to stop him, Tullamore reached his hand into the small floating basin and drank the rest of the water, leaving it empty. A few seconds after the last of the water had been drunk, the basin vanished and was replaced with a small stone effigy.

"Now, what answers do you seek?" asked the voice.

"We need to know the location of the land beyond the endless sea." Asked Jareth

"Very well, the answer you seek will be given." Said the voice.

Suddenly, the location of the land was known to Jareth, he knew exactly where to go. It was like magic.

"Thank you" said Jareth. No sooner than he finished talking, part of the base of the fountain crumbled away, leaving an odd-shaped hole. Yojano noticed the hole and effigy seemed to be of the same shape. He went to reach for it when the voice hissed at him.

"NOOO, it must be the other" the voice said as Tullamore approached the effigy. He picked it up and placed it in the hole. It settled and shifted back, locking itself into its new home. The water within the basin began to drain and the voice spoke:

"Thank you."

Moments later, the lights on the fountain turned off, leaving the three men shrouded in total darkness once again.

"I know where we must go, we need to get out of here." Said Jareth.

The three men set off at once. They were making better progress than before, but it did not seem quick enough. If they could just get out of there, Jareth could see his parents again, Yojano could reunite with his old friend Stromvir, and all would be well with the world.

After a few hours, it was evident they had taken a wrong turn as they were now lost. They walked for a few more hours when Jareth called for Yojano to come to him.

"I think you shall want to see this" he said.

Yojano made his way over to Jareth who was standing at the foot of a large fallen tree trunk, at his feet a skeleton rested. A skeleton who was fully clothed with a sword at his side, had evidently propped himself against the trunk of the tree and passed on some time ago. Yojano pulled at the clothes he was wearing when he noticed how familiar the clothing and sword looked. It was too dark to see any of his features clearly.

Jareth turned around to look for something, it was apparent he had found it when he began running towards a small section of the forest that appeared to have a less thick canopy, as there was some small amount of light hitting the forest floor. Jareth stood under the light for a few moments when the Sun Pendant flickered on. It was not strong, but it was light. He directed the light at the skeleton that lay at Yojano's feet. Yojano's eyes filled with tears at the sight.

The skeleton was that of Yojano's father, who had sacrificed himself to save his only remaining son, or so he thought. Yojano knelt and began searching his father for anything that may prove useful. However aside from the sword, he found nothing. He picked up his father's sword, which was miraculously undamaged. Yojano, who seemed to now know where he was going, led them out of the forest.

"Tullamore, how are you feeling?" asked Yojano

"I feel fine..why do you ask?" Tullamore asked.

"No reason, just checking" he said. "Jareth, we leave at dawn."

Jareth gave a nod and began arranging a place for them to sleep. They all turned in early that night, for they had an even longer journey ahead of them the next day.

CHAPTER 11
CENTAURIA AGAIN

Stromvir and Jarena were following the three leaders down a well-worn path through the woods. These woods were filled with the trees that Stromvir had seen in his dreams, and he recognized the landscape as the place he had been in his dream. He wondered though, how he was able to dream about this place despite never having been here. They continued to follow for a while and eventually Stromvir noticed something in the distance. It was the cave he had encountered in his nightmare. He began to worry they were being led to their own slaughter.

Stromvir halted in his path and his wife and the few people from the crew that came along followed his lead. The three leaders got some distance ahead before they noticed he had stopped. Argosh approached them and began to speak.

"I know of your concerns, Stromvir. Perhaps I am the one that caused those concerns." Said Argosh.

"What do you mean?" asked Stromvir.

"Well, I'm guessing you fear this cave? You saw it in a dream, did you not? A dream meant to drive you away from this place." Replied Argosh.

"How did you..?" asked Stromvir, looking very confused.

"We are the ones that caused the turmoil on your journey here. We have defenses in place to deter people from getting to Centauria. Those skilled enough to overcome them are granted entry. All of your questions will be answered in time." Said Argosh, reassuringly. Octavia and Resnik both gave agreeable nods.

Everyone continued down the path toward the cave, and when they reached the cave the three leaders led everyone inside and down through windy paths that seemed to become narrower as they progressed. Eventually they came to a large opening in the cave where the sun shone through, and there was a small stream running next to where they stood. In the center of the room was an altar of some sort. The water from the stream was zig zagging its way through a maze of slots cut into the ground at the base of the altar.

"When our ancestors came here, they were in danger. They were being hunted by the people of Gremela, simply because we are different. Most people could use magic back then, but we were cast aside because our magic is different, more powerful than that of a human wizard." Argosh said as he began pacing around the cave.

"They combined their magic into this basin, and from here, can control the magic of the land." Said Argosh. "You are the first to pass our trials, you have a home in Centauria for as long as you wish."

Argosh and the other leaders turned and took their respective places around the altar. They all raised their hands and began muttering an incantation. The water inside the basin began swirling and turned red, then blue, then a silvery white, and finally, it went back to clear.

The three leaders lowered their hands and made their way back to where Stromvir and his group stood.

"We have lifted the trials for those who hail from Gremela. Gremelan's are granted free passage to Centauria." Said Argosh.

"How do we get back? Our ship is destroyed." Asked Stromvir.

"There is an altar, identical to this one that controls the magic of Gremela, somewhere in the north of the empire. Using the magic of this altar, you can travel there." replied Argosh.

Stromvir and Jarena looked at each other with faces of wonder and excitement. They had never witnessed magic before, and seeing it now was a sight to behold. They had so many questions for Argosh and the others, but they knew there would come a time and place to ask them.

"Argosh, magic was banished over two thousand years ago. Are you quite sure there is an altar? If it was still around, would we not still have magic?" asked Stromvir warily.

"Banished? I have never heard of such a thing in all my life. Who would want to banish magic?" asked Argosh

"Cowards." Replied Resnik with contempt in his voice. "Those Gremelan's were always scared of us, they'da killed us all if it was upta them"

"Enough Resnik" said Argosh and Resnik bowed his head and shook it solemnly.

The group stood in silence for a few moments, pondering all the possibilities of why this had been done, who had done it, and where the altar was. If they could possibly undo what was done all those years ago, Gremela could be an even better place than it already was.

"Well, you said we can travel there? Let's go!" said Stromvir with excitement in his voice.

The three Centaurians gathered in a circle and motioned for the rest of the group to join hands with them. Shortly after they began muttering an incantation, before long the room started spinning, the group was hurled into the air. As if a tornado had ripped through the cave when suddenly, they were back in the cave, standing on solid ground, holding hands around the altar.

"What happened?" said Stromvir, perplexed and nauseated after what had just happened.

"I am..unsure.." responded Argosh, as he began looking at the altar in bewilderment. The water in the altar began to swirl once more, turning an array of different colors. This time it began splashing and spilling over the edges. When it stopped, there was a reflection on the surface of the water. The reflection was that of a large white stone structure, that appeared to be in the middle of the woods. The reflection was quite dark and difficult to make out, but Argosh and the others let out a shocked gasp simultaneously.

"The Malum Sepulcher" he said with fear in his voice. The three Centaurians immediately released their hold on each other and began to exit the cave at a run, without a word.

Stromvir and his crew began to follow immediately, he quickly learned that attempting to get an explanation was pointless, and their requests for answers were ignored. They continued following them for what seemed like ages. They had been making their way through a thick forest, much like the one in Gremela, but this one was not dark, it was as if the canopy of trees overhead did nothing to stop the light from penetrating to illuminate the forest floor. After several hours they came to a small opening in the forest that contained a large stone structure like the one in the picture. This one was different though, it was lit up with brilliant blue light, the light was emitting from the water in the center of the structure, which turned out to be a fountain.

"I do not understand…." Said Octavia and Argosh at almost the same instant.

"The reflection in the altar looked dark, as if the lights had gone out" continued Argosh looking at the rest of the group.

"What does that mean? What is this?" asked Stromvir, who saw the terror on their faces as they continued investigating the fountain.

"This is the Malum Sepulcher, it is what keeps evil out of this land. We swore to protect it as long as we could." Said Argosh who looked panicked.

"This one looks different from the reflection." said Stromvir.

"Indeed it does, but then, what was reflecting in the water?" Argosh asked himself as he gave Octavia a concerned look. They all stood in silence once again for a moment that seemed like hours, waiting for someone or something to break the silence. Argosh, Octavia and Resnik huddled together to discuss the matter, and were very secretive about it. Finally, Argosh turned to face the others.

"Have you ever seen anything like this in Gremela? It is likely there is one identical to this somewhere within the empire, keeping the evil within Gremela contained." Argosh stated confidently.

"We have never seen one, but what exactly do you mean by evil?" asked Stromvir.

"That is an excellent question, and one I do not have the answer to. We do not know exactly what happened once our ancestors arrived here. The details have unfortunately been lost throughout the generations. What we do know is shortly after they arrived here, there was said to have been a bright flash in the night sky and the next day, they found this. We do not know how they found out what they had to do, but they did it, and every generation since has continued." Said Argosh.

Suddenly, a small voice from Stromvir's group spoke up from the back.

"There is one, I have seen it. I drank from it." Said Kol apprehensively.

"You what?" asked Argosh as his face went blank and skin white as snow.

"I drank from it, nothing happened but me not knowing who or where I was, and not being able to walk or do much of anything for a few days, and when we exited the forest, we were on the other side of the empire, over a hundred miles away." Kol said as he began to recite the entire story of what happened that day with his brother.

"After you drank, did the lights burn out?" asked Argosh, concerned.

"No, but the voice that spoke to us tried to get us to drink from it again, but we refused. We barely made it out of that forest alive." Kol stated, starting to remember more of the details of that day. This information was clearly not what Argosh or the others wanted to hear. Argosh looked genuinely afraid and was visibly anxious.

"I need a word with Octavia and Resnik, if you please." Said Argosh.

Stromvir flashed Argosh a quick nod, and the three centaurians retreated a short distance to engage in this private conversation that Stromvir and his crew were not worthy of hearing. This annoyed Stromvir as he realized that whatever was happening, they were now all in this together.

After a short while, Argosh and the others came back and joined the rest of the group. They appeared slightly crestfallen. It was clear the news they were about to deliver was likely going to be far from good.

"We believe, that perhaps the fountain we saw reflected in the water was an identical one to this one, somewhere deep in the forests of Gremela." Said Argosh as he looked toward Octavia to continue.

"Many years ago, we were visited by a man from the neighboring empire of Cratemer. We have no quarrels with them, so they are granted a much easier entry into our land." Octavia continued. "We have told him the same things we have told you, and he saw our altar. He said that Cratemer also has an altar that controls the magic, and a Malum Sepulcher. He told us that the Malum Sepulcher of Cratemer is under heavy, nearly impenetrable guard." Octavia walked nearer to Stromvir, joined by Argosh and Resnik.

"Our friend, we fear that may have been the Malum Sepulcher of Gremela we saw. We were trying to travel there when it happened." Said Argosh solemnly.

"What does this mean?" asked Stromvir, who was still a little confused.

"It would seem, somehow, someone in Gremela has turned off the Malum Sepulcher, releasing the evil within Gremela. We fear that this was done, perhaps, on accident." Octavia answered with concern in her voice.

Just then, a loud bang came from across the field. Everyone looked up to see that a much smaller Centaur was running into the field where they all stood.

Panting and out of breath, the centaur spoke:

"Argosh, sir, three newcomers have shown up. I came for you as fast I could" said the centaur.

"Who are they?" replied Argosh.

"I am unsure, they just sort of, appeared from thin air. They did not come from the sea."

"My friend, I do believe the pixie you sent worked." Argosh said as he put a hand on Stromvir's shoulder.

"We will continue to discuss this problem later, now, we must greet our visitors." He said as he began to walk out of the cave, motioning for everyone to follow him.

CHAPTER 12

THE EVIL WITHIN

In a large room deep within a cavern sat a large stone effigy with a sarcophagus at the base, and a large perfectly round table with hundreds of grooves and drawings etched upon the surface. Just beyond the table was a small pool of water with a ball of dark purple light floating just above the surface. The ball of purple light began to pulsate and released a plume of smoke into the air above it, and the smoke formed a picture. A picture of a man surrounded by blue light, kneeling over to drink from a pool of water.

The blue light shrouding the man vanished, and the man joined two others and walked out of view. Moments after the three men disappeared, the ball of purple light started to pulsate once more. It began moving slowly toward the stone effigy and the sarcophagus. It hovered above the sarcophagus for a few moments before it cracked open to reveal an old man, dressed neatly in deep purple robes with a long grey braided beard. The purple light took shape of a person and floated down into the man inside the sarcophagus.

At once, the man inside the sarcophagus was lifted into the air, and a swirl of blue and red lights were engulfing him. After several moments of this, he was slowly lowered onto the ground beneath him.

The man, unsure of his own capabilities began walking slowly, putting one foot in front of the other. After a few steps he gathered himself and was stable enough to move about freely. He began inspecting his surroundings carefully, he had no idea where he was or why he woke up here.

After a few minutes, he found a very ornate looking staff leaned against the wall, not far from where he was entombed. He took the staff, something was telling him it was his. When his hand wrapped around the handle he felt a strong surge throughout his body, like the staff had filled him with life. He was still very weak, but now would be able to leave this place. He needed to find a way out, although he was unsure if there was one.

The place he was in was very large, but there seemed to be no obvious way out. He knew he was underground, which made escaping seem that much more difficult. He looked around every corner of the room for a conceivable way out, but there was nothing.. Gripping his staff firmly, he pointed it and let out a deafening scream of anger. A yellow and red stream of light flew from the end of his staff and hit the wall with a crash. The stone wall on the receiving end of the blast was cracked open, revealing a narrow passageway.

The man, although weary, made his way into the passage and continued along it. It got narrower as it went and eventually, he was forced to shuffle sideways and squeeze himself between the stones. He was having difficulty breathing with the tightness of the passage. He was beginning to wonder if coming this way was the right decision, even though he really did not have another choice. It was pitch black as well, he could barely see his hand in front of his face. He was making minimal progress but was determined to continue.

He came to a point where he felt he could no longer continue, but as that feeling reached its strongest, he noticed a small beam of light from ahead. It was barely noticeable, and it provided no extra light in his immediate surroundings. He pressed on through the pain and lack of air and eventually collapsed into an opening he did not realize was there. It was so dark, he had no idea where he was anymore. He could see the light in the distance and began slowly making his way towards it, making sure to check his surroundings and ensure he had proper footing before each step.

He began remembering fragments of things from before he was entombed. He tried to piece together these fragments into coherent thoughts but was struggling to make sense of it. One word suddenly came to his mind as the thoughts inside his head began to swirl out of control. In desperation he stamped his staff on the ground and shouted:

"LUX!"

With that, the brightest ball of pure white light burst from the tip of his staff and flooded the cave in which he stood. He stood in the now fully illuminated cave, which contained a shallow pool of captivating blue water. He suddenly developed an undeniable thrust, which the blue water was unable to quench no matter how much he drank. He drank his fill and resumed making his way through the cave. He started making his way across the cave when he noticed several man-made statues and stone carvings toppled over and destroyed. There must have been a struggle here, these statues were reminiscent of a courtyard.

"Someone must have lived here" he said to himself as he passed the remains of a makeshift stone shelter. The contents of which were scattered about, and a trunk hidden beneath an ornate wooden bed lay broken open and contained only a book. He knelt to pick up the book, which had a singular world emblazoned upon the front:

Magideus

"Magideus?" the man muttered to himself. He shut the book and carried it with him back into the courtyard. He tucked the book into the pocket of his deep purple robes and continued searching for an exit. He walked to the far end of the courtyard, the spot where the tiny speck of light was visible when it was dark.

At the far end of the courtyard there was a large stone door hidden beneath a layer of thick, overgrown vines and moss. There was no discernible way of opening said door, it seemed to be shut tight. He looked around the walls and the floor and noticed a rough spot on the floor. It was a few feet away and was half hidden under a mass of roots from a nearby toppled tree. He attempted to shift the roots out of the way, but it was of no use, they were far too heavy.

He had a flash of memories again; they were beginning to cause him physical pain. Once again, a single word flashed across his mind:

"*Levare!*" he shouted, pointing his staff at the roots.

They lifted off the floor and were suspended in the air for a second. He was struggling to keep them up, they were too heavy for him. He was still weak but knew he needed to get out of this place. He dropped them and they landed with a loud crack, and the room shook.

Suddenly, a stone pedestal was rising out of the ground at his feet. The roots must have hit something when they fell. The pedestal in front of him was long and contained two metal arms rising just a few inches out from the base. He was unsure what to do, but he felt the urge to place his staff onto the pedestal. He placed his staff into the pedestal and almost immediately the floor directly in front of the door opened and an incomplete statue raised from the depths below. The statue was missing the person it was representing, instead, there was a singular staff standing on its own. The platform on which the staff stood appeared to once have a statue.

He suddenly had a thought and positioned himself next to the staff. Nothing happened, he tried repositioning himself slightly, thinking maybe he needed to be standing a certain way. After several failed attempts, he stood in frustration, knowing he was so close to the exit, but could not pass the final challenge to leave this place. He looked at the staff for a moment, and then it came to him. He stood facing the door and gripped the staff with his left hand. At first, it appeared nothing had happened, but after a few seconds the stone door began retracting into the wall and the stone staff transformed into a real one. The surge of power he felt was too powerful, this caused him to fall to his knees.

He remained on the ground for just a few moments before he was able to gather himself enough to stand. The power he felt was still overwhelming him, he began to feel ill and soon enough was brought to his knees once more. He let the power engulf him, he had an incredible pain in his head. He submitted to the pain for a moment, he saw himself, less emaciated and lying on a stone table. He was surrounded by five others. They were standing in a circle around him. The incantations they were muttering resulted in a dark purple ball of magic, which floated over and stopped just over a pool of water. The incantations stopped, the group reformed and began again. He saw himself being lowered into the sarcophagus and sealed away. The group muttered a few other things, and the room changed into what it was when he awoke. He couldn't be sure how long ago this was, or why he was sealed away.

The strength of the power was starting to subside. He stood up and knew he had to find those people. He needed to remember why. He realized he was remembering more and more with every passing minute. The memories were coming to him fast and fierce, his head was overwhelmed with fleeting images of his past, but the important images seemed to be absent.

With a newfound sense of purpose, he stood up and faced the bright light coming from the now opened door. He felt in his robes for the book he found, realizing it would be of great importance to him. He walked forward a few steps and after he was clear of the platform, a disembodied voice spoke to him:

"Goodbye, Magideus"

He paused for a moment and pulled out the book. He opened it and handwritten upon the first page was a name:

Lord Granok, Magideus

He suddenly remembered that name, it was his own. He was the Magideus, he was Lord Granok. He was still missing most of the important pieces of his memory. He knew his name, but not who he was.

He continued down the short path that led to the light outside. Upon taking a step outside he realized he was not underground, but he was at the top of a mountain. There was a small path that led down to the bottom, but it would take him days to get down from where he was. In the valley below him lay an immense lake, with a small island in the center. This lake seemed familiar, but he couldn't quite remember where he had seen it before. He stayed at the top of the mountain and took in his surroundings for a few minutes before he took a deep breath, looked down at the lake once more, and headed down the path in front of him.

CHAPTER 13

THE REUNION

Jareth stood on the beach of an unfamiliar land, accompanied by Yojano and Tullamore. They were all wondering where they had landed when they saw three figures standing in the distance. The figures were foreign and not known by any of the men. Yojano held a hand up as he stepped in front of the other two, taking the lead.

As the three men approached the dark figures ahead, they realized they were standing in front of a centaur, a unicorn, and a gnome.

"Follow my lead" said Yojano to the other two men. Jareth and Tullamore both gave a quick but understanding nod.

The two groups were standing within a few feet of one another when Yojano spoke:

"Hello, we come from Gremela. We are searching for two people, Stromvir and Jarena. We have reason to believe they landed here several years ago" Yojano said as he pointed to the remains of an immense dilapidated ship in the distance, a ship he recognized as the Mare Domitor.

The Centaur stepped forward and examined the three men carefully, and he determined them to be truthful.

"Hello, I am Argosh, this is Octavia, and this is Resnik" he said as he pointed to each respective introduction. "Stromvir and Jarena indeed arrived here, but it was not years ago. It was just a few days ago." He continued.

Yojano looked deeply puzzled. He looked at Jareth and Tullamore before speaking again.

"You mean to tell me, it took them twenty-seven years to arrive here?" he asked, concerned.

Just then, two more figures emerged from the distance and came into view. They were human, and Yojano instantly recognized them as Stromvir and Jarena, and he broke down into tears. Jareth stood staring at the people he assumed were his parents, and he immediately recognized his father as their likeness to each other was strong.

"Jareth.." said Jarena as she too broke down into tears, and began a full sprint towards her son, who was now an adult and no longer the small boy she regrettably left behind. She could not contain herself; she was overcome with emotions and tears. She was clutching Jareth when Stromvir made his way to them as well. Tears were swelling in everyone's eyes at the reunion.

"Mother…father…" said Jareth. He could not believe his eyes, the people he assumed were dead were standing before him, seemingly more alive than ever. The tears continued for some time, and when everyone seemed to be gathering themselves, Argosh spoke.

"We are glad you are here. Which one of you is the Emperor?" asked Argosh.

"I am." Said Yojano as he stepped toward Argosh and shook his hand. "Yojano, this is Jareth, and this is Tullamore. We mean you no harm" he assured them.

"We know, we have been filled in by Stromvir and his crew. We have much to discuss. Follow us." Argosh said as he motioned for everyone to follow him further inland.

Everyone began to follow him as he led them back into the clearing that contained the Malum Sepulcher.

Argosh recited everything he had told Stromvir and his crew previously.

Jareth, Tullamore, and Yojano looked horrified. They had just come from this place within Gremela, had it been them that released the evil? But the bigger question, what was the evil?

"I drank from the fountain." Tullamore volunteered this information, he seemed to think it was important. "There was a small basin floating in the water, containing the same water it was floating in. I drank the water that was remaining in the floating basin, and after that the base of the fountain began to crumble, and a small stone effigy appeared in place of the floating basin."

"And after that?" Argosh asked anxiously.

Jareth and Tullamore looked at one another before Tullamore spoke up:

"I placed the effigy within the fountain, the voice thanked me and the light vanished." Said a very crestfallen Tullamore.

Argosh and Octavia looked at each other in horror. Resnik muttered something under his breath, walked over to a nearby tree and sat down at the base with his head in his hands.

"Can you take us there?" Argosh asked Jareth.

"I can. We can be there in a few moments. I am ready when everyone else is." Said Jareth as he looked around at everyone.

"I shall return shortly, my kind need me." Said Octavia as she vanished into thin air. The group gathered their belongings to prepare for their trip. They had no idea how long they would be in Gremela for. Argosh and Resnik also left to inform their kinds about what was happening. Argosh, Resnik, and Octavia were the three leaders of Centauria, but each one of them also led their own kind.

An hour had passed when Argosh and Resnik had returned and were prepared to leave. Jareth was a little apprehensive about this journey as he had never taken this many people at once. Jareth was leaning against a nearby tree when Stromvir and Jarena approached him.

"My son, there are no words that can explain what we did. I hope in time, you can forgive us. We were trying to make a better life for you" said Stromvir as Jarena clutched his arm, doing her best to hold back tears.

"Leaving without you was my biggest regret, and I did not make the decision lightly. Deep down I think we were unsure if we would make it back, we did not want to risk your life as well" said Jarena through a veil of tears. She let go of Stromvir's arm and lunged at Jareth, wrapping her arms around him in a warm embrace. Jareth struggled to hold back his own tears as well.

"Mother, Father, I am sure you have your reasons for doing what you did. I am glad you are alive, and even though I am no longer a child, I could not be happier that I get to know you now. If only Uncle Dravin had lived long enough to see you again" said Jareth as he lowered his head in sorrow.

"My brother…is dead?" asked Stromvir who had a newfound look of sadness in his eyes.

"He died a while ago. It was just me and Karavena for a while, until I was chosen." Jareth explained.

Stromvir and Jarena looked at each other with hopefulness in their eyes.

"Karavena?" asked Jarena with a smile on her face.

"Dravin's daughter. When I was six, he had a daughter of his own." Jareth said.

Stromvir began to say something but was interrupted by a loud bang, which turned out to be Octavia returning. She had appeared from thin air and landed in the exact spot she was in when she left.

"I am ready, shall we go?" she asked as everyone looked at her.

"I believe we are ready" stated Argosh

"Once we arrive, what is the plan?" asked Yojano.

"We are going to see the Malum Sepulcher. Then we will likely need to find the altar that contains Gremela's magic. All we know is it somewhere in the north of the empire." Explained Argosh.

Yojano stood looking puzzled for a moment before realizing that he perhaps had an idea of where they could start.

"I think I may know of a place to start." He said.

"Sir?" asked Argosh.

"There is a city in the north called Haven, it is on the coast of the endless sea. Just off the coast, there is an island that is home to an inactive Volcano. The volcano is said to have become dormant around the same time the magic was banished. I find it hard to believe that is mere coincidence."

"Yojano, that is where Diomede lived, correct?" asked Jareth.

Yojano nodded his head in agreement.

"Pardon me, but who is Diomede?" asked Octavia. Argosh and Resnik nodded in agreement, as if they too were curious about Diomede.

"He is my brother. He tried to kill me and take over Gremela, but fortunately for me Jareth here was able to stop him."

"What happened to him?" asked Argosh.

"I took him to the Sol Carcerem. A prison for the wayward souls of the universe." Said Jareth. "I don't believe he will be of any danger to us any longer."

The group looked around at each other for a few moments before gathering themselves into a small circle around Jareth.

"Yojano, grab onto my shoulder. Everyone else, grab onto Yojano or someone who is touching him." Jareth instructed. "And hold on tight, the sensation tends to make first timers a little ill, but do not worry, it will be over in a moment." Jareth explained further.

Jareth rotated the Sun Pendant, and it began to emit a thin streak of the brightest white light anyone had ever seen.

"Is everyone ready?" he asked.

One by one everyone in the group nodded. Moments later everyone felt themselves lift off the ground and shoot forward at a dizzying speed, their vision became blurred, the noise rattled their ears, and they all felt compressed as if traveling through a hollow reed. No more than a few moments later everyone felt their feet touch the ground and they were in the middle of a thick dark forest, shrouded in complete darkness.

CHAPTER 14

THE COUNCIL

It was darker than night, Resnik could barely see his hand in front of his face.

"Ayeee, it's too dark here, what was ya' expectin' us to do in complete darkness?" Resnik said as he stumbled around, trying to find his footing. He continued to complain about the darkness, much to the chagrin of the others.

"Oh will you knock it off Resnik, none of us can see!" Argosh said sternly. Resnik muttered something to himself and took a few steps in the opposite direction.

Suddenly there was a small ball of light floating in the center of where they all stood. The group looked up to see Jareth standing a little way into the forest where a tiny speck of sunlight was penetrating the thick canopy above. He was turning his sun pendant and channeling the resulting light into the ball. Jareth made several more of these balls of light and sent them to points around where they were standing to illuminate the surrounding forest. The balls of light hung suspended in the air while the group looked around to discover the Malum Sepulcher.

Jareth, Yojano and Tullamore had just been here, but it could not have looked any different than what they remembered. They remembered a vast white marble fountain; with the bluest water they had ever seen and a bright blue light shrouding the fountain. However, now there was dark purple water spilling over the edges into a moat surrounding the fountain. The water seemed to move on its own accord. The tip of the fountain was emitting a dark purple light which was swirling around like a liquid in a freshly shaken bottle.

Tullamore slowly approached the fountain and leaned over the edge to get a closer look. He scooped some of the water up with his hand and it floated away like smoke from a fire. Before anyone had a chance to speak, he was knocked backward and sent soaring into a nearby tree.

Yojano ran to him at once only to discover he had been knocked unconscious and had a dark purple stain on his hand. With each passing moment the purple stain grew darker and larger until eventually it engulfed his entire hand. Tullamore began to stir and when he awoke, his eyes were filled with rage. Octavia galloped over at once to attend to his hand. Within a few seconds she had managed to prevent the stain from getting any larger but was unable to get rid of it completely.

"I have never seen this kind of magic before.." she said very concerned. Argosh and Resnik came to investigate and despite their efforts, nothing worked. Tullamore's hand appeared to be permanently darkened by the purple substance.

"Does it hurt?" asked Octavia.

"A bit, but I think I can manage." Tullamore said, his eyes were a little more relaxed now. He stood up and made his way to the rest of the group, who were all still standing and looking at the Malum Sepulcher in complete astonishment and bewilderment. Argosh and Octavia circled the great stone fountain for several minutes, ensuring they examined every inch of it.

Eventually, they rejoined the rest of the group and looked very concerned.

"I think we must go to the altar now." Argosh stated and Octavia nodded in agreement.

"Perhaps," Jareth interrupted. "we should visit the council, they may know more about this."

"The council?" Argosh asked.

"When I became the Solistima, there was a group of five individuals that referred to themselves as 'The Council'. They are the ones who made me the Solistima, they said they control the ebb and flow of the universe. If anyone knows what was contained in this, it will be them." Jareth explained.

"I agree with Jareth." Said Yojano "Visiting the altar is important, but unless we know what we must do there, the effort is pointless."

The three Centaurians looked at one another for a moment before finally nodding in agreement.

"Well then, The Council it is. Let us go, we are losing valuable time." Said Argosh.

Moments later, the group once again felt as if they were being forced through a hollow reed, and this time the sensation made Resnik quite sick upon landing back on the ground.

"Oyy, ya' could try to go a bit slower, dontcha think"? Resnik said as he retched from the feeling. The group stood on the edge of the Lake of Fears as Jareth pointed toward the island.

"That is where we must go" he explained.

Argosh looked confused and paused to look at the rest of the group before speaking.

"They are, in the water?" He asked, utterly bewildered. Jareth suddenly remembered that only members of the council, including himself, could see the island. He wondered if this was just an illusion caused by enchantments. He felt he should bring the group with him, but the risk of them falling into the lake of fears was not worth the outcome, so he decided he would return on his own.

"I will go alone, and I will relay all information I receive." He explained. The rest of the group set up camp, assuming it would take at least a few hours to find out what was happening. After camp was set up, Jareth took off for the island and vanished from sight.

Moments later he arrived on the island. After a short walk to the altar where he met the council, he found the place largely overgrown and seemingly abandoned. He cut the overgrown vines and bushes down to reveal the stone table at which he summoned the council the last time he was there. For a moment, he thought of the overnight wait he endured the last time while he waited for the sun to rise. He began to gather some materials for a makeshift bed when he remembered he could produce a small amount of sunlight at any moment. He dropped the sticks and leaves he had gathered and summoned a feeble beam of light from the sun pendant on his chest and aimed it at the table. At first it seemed the small amount he produced wasn't quite enough, but much like last time, the light began to fill the table and before long there were five figures standing before him in the exact same places they appeared last time.

"We know why you have summoned us here Solistima" the voice of Bashkar, God of the Seas said with a hint of concern.

"Tell me what is happening" Jareth demanded.

The five members of the council that stood before him exchanged worried looks and muttered amongst themselves before Krishna, the God of Mountains spoke.

"Long ago, there was a man by the name of Kolnir. He was a member of this very council. He oversaw the magic of this world, and he did his job well. He was known as The Magideus. During Mercado's reign of terror, the woman he loved was accidentally killed. From that moment, he was a changed man. He let his power overcome him. He was growing stronger, and his anger drove the strength, and the strength fueled his anger."

Krishna said. "One day, he approached us, telling us his plan. He was going to end Mercado's reign and exact his revenge, and he was going to do it at the expense of thousands of innocent lives."

Telgarna the Goddess of the Wind spoke up now.

"We tried to change his mind, but he told us there was nothing we could do to stop him. His face was full of rage and hatred at our refusal to help, and we knew the fate of the world was in our hands. We had to act. We summoned the Solistima down from a period of sleep and tasked him with stopping Mercado" She said solemnly. "When Kolnir found out what we had done, he became enraged. He began performing dark rituals all throughout Gremela, hundreds of people went missing, or were killed."

"I do not understand" Jareth said.

"You will in due course, Solistima" she replied.

"We were left with no choice. Using a combination of our powers and the magic that was still active in Gremela, we were able to seal him away in a deep sleep. There were risks of him being awoken, but the safety of the world far outweighed those risks." She continued.

Vranash, the God of Land took over for her as she gave him a nod.

"We constructed three Malum Sepulchers, and spread his essence between them. We placed his physical body inside a sarcophagus deep within Mount Carana." He said as he pointed to the tallest mountain on the horizon. "He carved out a cave inside the mountain, and lived there for several weeks, gaining power, before we were able to find him." He continued. "We set our plan in motion and were almost stopped by him and his small group of followers, but we were able to corner him inside the cave and perform the ritual needed to seal him away. He put up a great fight against us, there were a few moments where we began to think he might overpower us."

Jareth looked at the rest of The Council with great concern.

"Am I wrong in assuming the Magideus is now free once more?" Jareth asked.

The members of the council all bowed their heads in shame and responded with the answer Jareth already knew but did not want to admit.

"No" they all said in unison.

"How has this happened?" Jareth asked.

"There are always unforeseen flaws in these rituals. We split his essence into three equal parts and contained each part in a separate Sepulcher. Since his essence, his life force was trapped inside the Sepulcher, it was almost as if he was still alive, just not physically." Krishna explained.

"It is because of him that the last Solistima disappeared. He knew the Solistima was the only one capable of defeating him. We are unsure of what happened to your predecessor, but what we do know is that Lord Granok destroyed him." Krishna explained further. "It was at that moment we knew what we must do. We performed the ritual and after we stopped the flow of magic from the Altar, preventing the inhabitants of Gremela from using magic."

Jareth let this information sink in for a minute before he asked any further questions. He was unsure of what to make of this, he was confused and scared, the latter of which being an emotion he hadn't felt in some time. Could he really be stopped by this man? Where was he? How would he stop him? All of these questions swam around in his head and overwhelmed him.

"We believe that a small amount of his essence was removed from the Malum Sepulcher in Gremela, and we believe it is this that caused his awakening." Said Krishna.

"How do we stop him?" Jareth asked hopefully.

The council looked at one another and after a few moments of silence, Krishna spoke up once more:

"Solistima, there is no stopping him now. We must however, stop him from releasing his essence from the other two Sepulchers. That is essential.'" Krishna said. "If he manages to release the remaining essence, we fear we may be unable to defeat him, and the fate of our world will be in his hands." Krishna continued. "Solistima, it is your mission to ensure he does not find the other sepulchers."

"Where are they?" Jareth asked

"One is on Centauria, which we believe you have seen. And the other, well the other is deep within the Hallowed Forest in Cratemer." Krishna said as his voice trembled. "But first, go and release the magic of Gremela once more, but beware, doing so may cause some unwanted effects for a while, but fear not, everything will return to normal." Krishna stated.

"You must go, Solistima, we are counting on you! Go to Mount Karnath at once." Krishna said, and the others agreed.

Moments later they all grabbed hands and disappeared once more leaving Jareth there alone with his thoughts. He knew what he had to do, but how was he to do it? He sat on an old stump for a while looking up at the sun setting on the horizon and thought about what had just happened. He sat there until the sun had completely vanished over the horizon, he let the darkness settle over him, the cool night breeze hitting his face as he planned his next move.

CHAPTER 15

THE ALTAR

The next morning Jareth was awoken by a torrential downpour of rain. He was caught off guard but managed to gather himself quickly enough to avoid being completely drenched. He sat under a tree and ate an apple from a nearby apple tree before setting off for the mainland.

Once again, he took off with a flash of light into the constricting darkness, and moments later his feet touched solid ground. He was standing in the middle of the camp that was set up by the group to await his return. Everyone was sitting in one of the tents eating some Loxie Yojano caught.

"Oiii, this is far from delicious, don't you guys eat anything better?" asked Resnik contemptuously.

"Loxies are a staple of Gremela, and we all love them! If you are unhappy with it, you are more than welcome to gather your own food." Yojano said seriously.

"You might as well…" Resnik started but he was interrupted.

"Jareth!" exclaimed Yojano "What is happening?"

"Everyone stay seated, I have much to tell you. It is far worse than we thought." Jareth said looking at Yojano seriously. Jareth proceeded to tell them everything The Council had told him. Yojano was floored, he leaned down in his chair and placed his hands in his face and ran them through his thick red hair. The Centaurians looked positively terrified at the news. Octavia looked to Resnik, then to Argosh, then back again.

"What do we do?" asked Yojano.

"We need to go to the altar and restore Gremela's magic." Jareth said

"Did the council tell you where it is?" asked Argosh.

"Mount Karnath." He replied.

"Then we must go!" Said Yojano as he rallied the group.

Stromvir and Jarena were at a loss for words. Seeing their son possess such power and leadership brought tears to their eyes. The group ate a big meal before setting off for Mount Karnath, going on a journey like this on an empty stomach would likely cause many arguments along the way.

They all locked hands and Jareth took them into the constricting darkness once more. Resnik was none too pleased with this form of travel, but he did not have any better means, so he accepted it for what it was. Upon his feet touching the ground, Resnik stumbled into some nearby bushes and began retching.

"You will get used to the sensation before long" Jareth said to Resnik as he patted him on the shoulder. Resnik straightened himself and nodded to Jareth.

Jareth and the rest of the group were standing at the base of a large mountain with foothills on either side and large rock formations at the base. Behind where they stood was a tall ominous looking castle, with numerous turrets and towers.

"My brother's" Yojano said as he pointed at the castle. The group looked at one another before setting off on the trail leading to the base of the mountain.

"We must exercise caution." Yojano warned. "While inactive, this is still an ancient volcano. It could erupt at any moment. Let's do our best to keep our voices down."

The group walked down the trail for a while when they came to a small opening in the base of the volcano. It looked just big enough for one person to fit through at a time. Yojano shot Jareth a warning look before proceeding into the cave first. On his signal, the others snaked their way through the small opening one by one until everyone was inside. The cave was dark, damp, and smelled of mold. Much to everyone's surprise, there was more than enough room for everyone to move around without bumping into one another. They surveyed their surroundings in detail for several minutes before determining there was only way to go. In front of them there was a small path lined with rock on either side, it seemed to go on forever.

After what seemed like an hour, but was only a few minutes, they came to an opening in the path that led to a cavern. The cavern in which they stood was monumental. There were stalactites and stalagmites all over. A small pool of water filled by a rushing waterfall above dominated the center of the room. The room seemed empty for the most part, and on the far side of the room the group saw yet another opening.

"Stay close together" Yojano warned them. "If someone or something has beat us here, I am certain they will not be friendly."

Jarena looked at Stromvir with pure fear in her eyes. She was not prepared for what was to come next. Stromvir could sense this and placed his hand on her shoulder and pulled her in for a warm embrace before they continued. As they walked, he gripped her hand tightly and drew his sword with his free hand. Yojano, Argosh, Jareth and Resnik all drew their weapons as well.

They made their way through the second opening and were once again walking down a narrow stone lined path. The ceiling was high, and the walls seemed to be closing in and before long they all struggled to fit down the path. They were all forced to turn sideways and shuffle down the path one at a time.

Upon reaching the end of the path they found themselves in a cavern once again. This cavern was much different than the other, much larger, and there seemed to be light coming from underneath. At the far end of this cavern there was a large stone object with a bright pulsating light emitting from the center. Jareth noticed that not ten feet in front of them, the ground of the cavern was gone. They were standing on the edge of a large pit. Jareth peered over the edge to discover that the pit was extraordinarily deep and was filled with burning hot magma that was bubbling and gurgling. Stromvir pointed out that there was a narrow path leading to the stone object.

"I think we can.." Stromvir said but was interrupted by a deafening crack. Suddenly, everyone looked toward the stone object to see a tall man with robes of deep purple approaching the stone object. The man stood over the object and peered into it for several seconds before reaching in with both hands and pulling out a large stone. He heaved the stone over the side of the pit and the group watched it plummet down into the pit, sizzling when it hit the magma.

Just then, the pulsating light coming from the stone object grew infinitely brighter. The stone object appeared to have a brilliant silver liquid flowing over the edges now. The liquid kept flowing and eventually spilled over the side of the pit and down into the magma. Eventually the liquid from the stone object was filling the pit below, which was swirling and sizzling with great intensity now. Jareth noticed the ground starting to shake and the narrow path that led to the stone object, which

Jareth now realized was the Altar he was looking for, started to crumble away into the pit below.

The room was well lit now, and they could see their surroundings without difficulty. The man next to the altar looked deranged, like he had an unyielding sense of sinister purpose. He looked up from the Altar and noticed the group standing on the opposite side of the pit. The look on his face was nothing short of fury. Before anyone in the group could think of how to react, the man in the purple robes raised a staff and shouted. Suddenly, there was a beam of yellow and red light flying towards them. Everyone in the group managed to duck out of the way just in time, and the spell hit the stone wall behind them and left a small hole. Jareth was the first one to stand up and when he did, he noticed the man looking at him with rage in his eyes. At that moment, a disembodied voice spoke to Jareth and only Jareth.

"Solistima.." and Jareth felt the Sun Pendant vibrate as if it were fighting off an invisible force. He closed his robes over the sun pendant, he noticed above him was the opening of the volcano, and the sun was blaring down on them, without a word he grabbed everyone and took off into the compressing darkness once more. Seconds after they vanished from the cavern, the entire cavern started to collapse and fall into the pit. Their feet hit solid ground outside of the cave they entered, and they were back at the base of the volcano.

"Is everyone okay?" Asked Jareth

"Jareth what happened?!" asked Yojano seriously.

Jareth was on his knees clutching the sun pendant as though it were causing him great pain.

"Nothing, I am fine, but I knew we had to get out of there." He said.

At that moment, everyone heard a beautiful noise, a song coming from the sky. They looked up to find a beautiful red and orange Phoenix flying above them. In their haste to leave they never noticed that the volcano had started erupting, sending fragments of searing hot rock and lava down the mountain toward them. The Phoenix began swooping down and letting out heavy breaths which turned the lava into stone almost instantly.

"The phoenix again…" said Stromvir.

Stromvir noticed Jareth giving him a puzzled look.

"When we were traveling to Centauria, we were saved by that Phoenix, it got us to where we needed to go after closing a rift in the sea." Stromvir explained.

After several minutes of the Phoenix flying and swooping down to stop the lava, it flew over the crest of the mountain and out of sight. It was at that moment they realized they had left someone in the cavern.

"Where is Octavia?!" shouted Argosh.

The group looked around, and immediately Jareth started to run back inside the cavern, but he was knocked backward seconds before he entered.

Octavia came galloping out of the cave at full speed, barely managing to stop before she reached the group. Within moments the chaotic scene around them had shifted, and it suddenly began to storm heavier than it ever had before. There was so much rain the ground could not absorb it fast enough and soon they were ankle deep in water.

The weather kept drastically changing every few minutes without warning. After the rain, the sun came out and gave off a burning heat that no one had ever felt before. Just as the heat became unbearable, the weather shifted once more, and it began to snow and before long there was several inches of snow all around them.

"These must be the effects the council was speaking of" said Jareth calmly.

"Do explain." Said Yojano as he raised one eyebrow with curiosity.

"The council told me that restoring the magic may result in some 'effects'. They said not to worry, once everything settled it will return to normal." Jareth explained.

The group stood at the base of the mountain in awe of what was happening when suddenly they noticed the trees in the distance shrinking and growing rapidly, the bushes were changing color, and the small wildlife was growing bigger and then smaller. The sun was moving all around, and the two moons appeared in the daytime sky.

Suddenly Yojano, Stromvir and Jarena became very ill. They fell to their knees and were retching uncontrollably. The rest of the group did what they could to help, but it was no use.

"I think the magic has been released once again. I fear we may have been too late." Jareth said as he bowed his head in defeat.

Jareth looked into the distance and saw a large brown bear walking along the edge of a lake, and suddenly the bear turned into a lion, then a sheep, then a rabbit. Finally, after taking notice of this Octavia stood up.

"It's a shapeshifter!" she exclaimed.

"A what?" asked Yojano.

"A shapeshifter, a creature or person that can change their form at will." She continued. "I do believe you are correct Jareth, the magic has been released. If what the council told you is true, we must return to Centauria at once to ensure the safety of our Sepulcher." She stated, and Argosh and Resnik agreed.

"We shall return shortly" Argosh said . Resnik clambered onto Octavia's back, and the three of them vanished.

CHAPTER 16

THE MAGIDEUS

The man in deep purple robes stood at the foot of a large mountain, a clear reflective lake in front of him. The lake reflected a nearly perfect image of the mountain. He approached the water and peered back at his own reflection and was disgusted by what he saw. A pale, wrinkly, sickly-looking man with a very unkempt beard that was far too long. His thick, untidy hair made it hard for him to see, as the wind was constantly blowing it all around. He was weak, very hungry, thirsty, and felt he would collapse at any moment. He desperately made his way to the edge of the water and knelt to drink. He drank and drank, never once considering when he might stop.

After he drank his fill, he raised his head away from the water and as he was turning away, he noticed the bush some ten feet from him was full of bright red berries. He remembered these berries, he remembered they could be eaten. He had eaten them before, he knew it. He hurried toward the bush in desperation and seized one handful of berries after the other, proceeding to stuff them in his mouth to eat after each handful. Some of the color was beginning to return to his face, the berries gave him a sudden jolt of energy. He took advantage of this and continued walking along the shore of the great lake before him. Eventually he came to a large beach which had two great trees growing on either end. He stood on the beach and gazed across the lake in astonishment when he noticed a small island, way out in the center of the lake. It was too far to swim, he had no boat, but for some reason, he was drawn to this island.

He began searching for anything he could use to make a boat, but there was nothing good enough for that. He sat looking at the island for some time, wondering how to get there, wondering *what* was there. At that moment, there was a bright pillar of light coming down from the sky into the center of the island. No more than a moment later, the pillar of light disappeared, and a shockwave knocked him backward into a tree, rendering him unconscious.

He awoke and sat up slowly a few moments later. He tried to get to his feet, but he was too weak, his legs seemed to be paralyzed. He tried with all his might to move them an inch and they would not budge. Desperate, he began dragging himself to the water for a drink, he was suddenly overcome with thirst. With one great final heave he landed headfirst into the water and began to drink. After a few desperate gulps of water, he had a memory flash into his head so violently he raised his head in horror and let out a scream.

He was suddenly in a dark forest, a forest so dark one could barely see their hand in front of their face. This memory seemed quite different, as if it were someone else's. He spun around to look at his surroundings. In the distance he saw a brilliant blue light shining through the darkness. He made his way toward it, tripped and fumbling over tree stumps and bushes every few feet. As he got closer to the light, he noticed there were five people standing in a circle around a small ball of blue light that hung suspended in the air. He realized quickly that whoever was in this memory could not hear him, as he was already making an awful lot of noise, and no one seemed to notice. Moments later, the five people raised their hands above their heads, and with them raised a majestic white marble feature. They muttered an incantation in a language unknown to the man, but it sounded as though a ritual was being performed.

The man watched on as they continued their incantation, which seemed to be of great complexity. They lowered their arms and became silent. The man looked at the stone feature and suddenly realized how familiar it was, but he did not understand why. He did, however, understand with absolute certainty that he was looking at a great white marble fountain. He continued watching, the five people had taken a few steps into the forest and were carrying something back to the fountain. They placed it at the base of the fountain and three of them began muttering another incantation. This one resulted in the fountain being filled with the purest blue water he could ever remember seeing. They picked up the mysterious object from the ground and threw it in the water, and as it fell from their arms he saw the figure of a man, and within seconds, the water started to swirl and swell. Whoever was thrown into the water began shaking violently and a dark purple substance, neither liquid nor gas, came rising out of them.

Two of the people gathered some of the purple substance into smaller basins of their own, and within a few moments had vanished. The remaining substance still floating in the air above the water was suddenly plunged into the water, which began to swirl and shake more violently than before, and then, it was calm. The Fountain began flowing and the water turned blue once more. The three people retrieved the human figure they threw into the fountain and began to walk away when suddenly it felt as though the man's head was pulled backward with great force, he was flipped over, thrown to the ground and shot through the air as if from a cannon. He was moving through the forest he was in at great speed; he was unable to control his movements, he was flying past trees and over rivers and rock formations and before long he was out of the forest and in a field, a field he recognized. He realized this was his homeland, he suddenly remembered everything about it.

Without warning he suddenly stopped and was back in front of the same group of five people, they were wearing midnight blue cloaks with matching hoods, their faces could not be seen. He had seen this memory before, not long after he had awoken from his long sleep. He attempted to piece things together but was having difficulty, there was so much missing from his memory. Something crucial, something that could be a matter of life and death. He was suddenly awoken with a jolt, and he was on the shore of the very same water he had plunged his head into just moments before. He stood up as he now had the strength he needed. He stood in silence for a while, thinking of what he had just seen. He began to piece a few things together. He was fairly certain the man that was plunged into the water was himself, and something important was taken from him. He felt the sudden uncontrollable need to find the fountain, return and take back what was his. Perhaps this would help him remember more about who he was, and why he was entombed all those years ago. He was not even sure how much time had passed since his entombment.

He knew he had great powers, for he was learning more and more about what he was capable of with every passing minute. After he almost completed his dangerous journey down the tall mountain, he learned for instance that he was able to disappear and reappear at will and could even reappear in different places. He simply needed to stamp his staff on the ground and imagine his destination and he would be there in an instant. He had never done this for a greater distance than just a few feet for he was unsure of his strength, he knew not whether attempting to reappear somewhere far away in his current weakened state would do him any favors. Knowing he had no choice, he focused on the only image of the fountain he had. He knew that when he arrived the five people whom encircled the fountain would likely not be present, having finished their job long ago. He closed his eyes, stamped his staff on the ground and instantly felt himself being pulled in many directions at once, he was flipping backwards and forwards, even sideways. He could not see or hear anything; it was a whirlwind of light and dark. There was a loud crack, and he suddenly felt his feet touch the ground.

He opened his eyes and saw the great white marble fountain before him. He was astonished at the power he possessed, but perhaps this power was normal for someone like him. He was still missing vital parts of his memory. He approached the fountain with great caution. He looked down at the fountain and saw the same swirling purple liquid the others had seen. It was spilling over the top into a small moat around the base. Examining it carefully, he dipped his hand in. Much to his surprise the liquid seemed to absorb into his hand, and the way it swirled intensified. He tried to pull his hand away, but the purple liquid seemed to be engulfing him. Before long, the liquid was swirling all around him and he was being lifted off his feet. He was approaching the dark purple ball of light emitting from the tip of the fountain. He felt himself getting closer to the light, its warmth was intensifying. He could see nothing but light, the purest, whitest light. The light slowly faded and he was lowered to the ground.

At that moment, a flood of memories hit him once more, he could feel himself being teleported through his own mind as he suddenly remembered nearly everything about his past. He saw himself as a teenager, a young boy, a younger man, and even himself during his entombment. He remembered talking to the travelers who sought information, he remembered more than he thought was possible, yet he still felt as though he were missing something. He saw a vast, ancient volcano, a stone altar at the heart. He knew without a doubt he needed to go there, he needed to find the altar. He took notice of the increase in strength he suddenly seemed to have. Taking advantage of this, without hesitation he stamped his staff on the ground and concentrated on his destination. Once again, he was being pulled in many directions at the same time, he felt his head and feet being pulled in opposite directions, as though he were about to be torn in half, when suddenly, his lungs expanded and filled with oxygen, as his feet and the rest of his body came to rest at their destination.

    He was standing in the heart of the volcano, a few feet from him stood a black stone figure. It had a cylindrical base with a large round basin on top. In the center of the basin was a large stone that seemed to be stopping the flow of some mysterious substance. He cannot be sure what drove him to do it, but at that moment he reached into the basin, removed the large stone, and heaved it over the edge into the chasm below. He watched as the silvery liquid flowed over the edge of the altar and over the sides of the stone and down into the chasm. As the silvery liquid reached the magma, he felt a surge of power overcome him. He felt as if his powers had been released. A memory flashed over him, he remembered the silvery liquid, it was the magical essence within Gremela. The essence he, as The Magideus was in control of. A smile of satisfaction creeped upon his face, and he looked across the chasm to find others, staring at him.

      He knew without a doubt these others were here to try to stop him, he did not know why, but he understood them to be his enemies. Without a moment's hesitation he pointed his staff at them and shouted. A jet of yellow and red light shot from the end of his staff and missed the group by inches. As the ground began to shake violently, he focused on the group and could see something around one of their necks, a necklace, a pendant perhaps. After a moment, a realization hit him, and he knew what this was. He reached out his hand and he heard his own voice speak.

      "Solistima.."

But who was the Solistima? Why was he drawn to this person? He was desperate for his memories to return. He needed answers. He knew he must continue down this path, a path which had no clear direction, merely a driving force propelling him along. Without a warning, the group across the chasm vanished without a trace. He stood there on edge of the collapsing stone gazing into the depths below when he was hit with a shockwave of memories which brought him to his knees. He saw a man in white and yellow robes standing before him, wearing the same pendant he just saw. This man was different, an older man. This man was escorting him to a stone room, barely conscious. He was slipping in and out of this memory and into another. The other memory was himself standing on a hill, overlooking a great towering castle, situated on the sea. He recognized this castle, as though he had been there before. His memory flashed again to him being dragged through a dark passage when suddenly they stopped, and he felt himself being lifted high into the air. He was flipped over onto his back and caught one final glimpse of the man with the pendant, the Solistima. He was there shortly before he was entombed, he had something to do with his unjust imprisonment. He was beginning to piece more things together when he was sent spinning back into the memory of the castle, this time he was closer, almost within reach when he awoke suddenly, he stood upright, knowing what he must do. He pictured the castle in his mind, he concentrated with all his power on the only image he had. He was hoping the unknown force that seemed to be propelling him through this journey would continue. He had no idea what came next, who's castle this was, why he needed to go there, or why the Solistima was involved in his entombment, and for that matter, who the Solistima was.

He stamped his staff on the ground and when he opened his eyes, he was standing on the hill from his dream, The Castle on the Sea in the distance. He was suddenly hit with even more memories, too many at once to even begin to comprehend. He remembered this castle, and who lived in it. A merciless ruler who was responsible for the death of the woman he loved, and who the council refused to help him get rid of. He cared not who the ruler was now, for this was his castle, and he would take it by force. He stamped his staff on the ground and muttered a short incantation, moments later a magical dome was placed around the perimeter of the castle. A greedy smile lined his face as he made his way down the hill and into the city, ready to claim what was his.

CHAPTER 17

THE MAGIC RETURNS

Over the next several hours, the effects of the magic being restored became more problematic than anything. Jareth was by the shore of a nearby lake fishing for some Loxies when suddenly, the bushes erupted in flames, scaring the fish away. No more than a few seconds later they extinguished themselves and returned to their previous state, as if nothing had happened. The sky was changing from blue to orange to yellow and back to blue. These effects were very disorienting for everyone. It seemed that even some of the wildlife took notice of things not being how they usually were.

The group decided to stay put and wait for the Centaurians to return. Jareth was standing on the edge of the lake by himself when Stromvir approached him.

"Everything will be alright, my son."

"I sure hope so. Father, the council told me about The Magideus. They told me he has been awakened, and they also told me he knows the Solistima is the only one that can defeat him. They said he destroyed the last Solistima." Jareth explained.

"My son, there is nothing to fear. When the time comes, you will know what to do. You have so far. Perhaps being the Solistima means more than you think it does." Said Stromvir as he placed a reassuring hand on Jareth's shoulder.

The two of them talked and shared stories of their past adventures, Stromvir told Jareth about the journey to Centauria in detail. Stromvir told him about the dream he had, something he had told no one else.

"I want you to have this, Jareth" Stromvir said.

He had reached inside his tunic and pulled out a small cylindrical object on a necklace chain. "I used this on our journey. Upon using it, the Phoenix from my dream erupted out of the sky and helped guide our ship pass safely."

Jareth accepted the gift from his father and placed it around his neck, letting it dangle in front of the sun pendant.

"Father, do you think the phoenix from earlier was the same one as before?" Jareth asked.

"I do." He replied "But I am unsure as to how. I cannot be sure how the magic of that whistle works, but I was told to only use it in the gravest of situations. I shall tell you to do the same, my son."

Jareth nodded and suggested they return to the group. They were on their way back when there was a deafening crack. They looked up to see Octavia, Argosh and Resnik had returned.

They hurried up the hill where the Centaurians had reappeared, they had a look of uncertainty upon their faces. Jareth knew stopping the Magideus was going to be a long and hard journey, but it was one he was prepared to take on with his friends.

"Is everything alright Argosh?" Yojano asked.

"For now, our Sepulcher is well protected. Jareth, did the council tell you where then Sepulcher in Cratemer is?" asked Argosh.

"Yes, in the Hallowed Forest"

Argosh turned to Resnik:

"Resnik, go now!"

Resnik turned and with a snap of his fingers he vanished from sight.

Before Argosh or Octavia could say anything, the weather changed drastically. The sky turned from a brilliant to a most ominous shade of dark purple, with slate-colored clouds looming overhead. The rain began falling, the thunder rolling, and the lightning striking everywhere it could.

"Jareth, let's get out of here!" Yojano shouted.

"Where do we go? What's the plan?" he asked.

For the first time in his life, Yojano did not have the answer. He had no plan. He was not prepared for this and did not have the foggiest idea of how to stop it. For the first time in a very long time, he was truly scared. The only place he could think of going was the Castle. From there, they could formulate a plan together.

"The castle!" Yojano shouted over the roar of the storm. He grabbed ahold of Jareth as did the rest of the group and moments later they were once again flying through the compressing darkness. Yojano felt it hard to catch his breath. Within moments, their feet touched the ground, but they were not at the castle. They were standing in an open field just north of the capital. The Castle on the Sea could be seen in the distance.

Yojano looked around to find Jareth doubled over panting heavily, as if completely out of breath.

"Jareth, what happened?" he asked.

"I am unsure, for some reason, we cannot travel past this point. There seems to be some sort of magical barrier blocking our way."

Yojano took a few steps forward to the point where Jareth indicated and much to everyone's surprise, he was able to continue past on foot. Jareth clicked open the sun pendant and shot a small beam of sunlight at the barrier. The sunlight bounced off and reflected into the sky. It seemed as if there was a barrier blocking the use of magic beyond that point.

Yojano had a bad feeling in the pit of his stomach, but he knew they must continue. He hurried on ahead, leaving the rest of the group to fall slightly behind. Jareth and the rest of the group hurried behind him. They continued on foot until they reached the capital, and when they reached the front gates, it appeared a battle had already started. They were too late, the Magideus had taken over the city. Yojano's eyes filled with rage upon seeing his city overrun, the citizens mostly dead, the animals fleeing in every direction, and most of the buildings were set ablaze. The raging storm outside seemed to have no effect on the fire.

The group stood in the middle of the city, unsure of what to do. Jareth, Yojano, Stromvir and Argosh all drew their weapons and made for the Castle. They pushed their way through the destroyed city until they reached the beach.

Yojano, upon seeing the castle, let out a wail of despair. His fists clenched around his father's sword, his eyes turned the color of scarlet, much like his brother and he ran toward the castle, clambering up the marble steps to the bridge.

"Yojano no!" yelled Jareth as he chased after him. "Argosh, Octavia, you come with me. Mom, Dad, Tullamore, you wait here!"

"I am coming with you, son!" Stromvir said as he followed Jareth. Jarena was not going to stay down here while her husband and son ran off to their certain death, and Tullamore agreed. Both waited a few moments before following the others up the stairs and onto the bridge.

Jareth and Yojano reached the end of the bridge and were standing in the courtyard when they saw a man standing on the far side, looking out at the sea. They had seen this man before, he was in robes of deep purple with long grey hair and a braided beard. He was the man they saw inside Mount Karnath. He was Lord Granok, The Magideus.

"What have you done?!" Yojano screamed, pure rage and hatred lining his face.

"What others have failed to do" he muttered. He turned to face Yojano and looked deep into his eyes, penetrating his very soul. "Worry not, Yojano, I shall find a place for you in my ranks."

He pointed his staff at Yojano and a spell shot in his direction. Yojano ducked out of the way of the spell just in time. Jareth gripped his sword ever tighter, and to his great relief, the sword became imbued with sunlight. He lunged for Lord Granok with a slash of his sword but was sent flying through the air, into a marble pillar.

"Ahh, I see the Solistima has returned once more." Lord Granok said as he moved closer to the unconscious Jareth. He stopped when he was standing directly over Jareth. "Pathetic" and he pointed his staff at Jareth and muttered:

"Surgere!"

Jareth sat straight up, the wind was knocked out of him, he gasped for air. Lord Granok kneeled so that he was face to face with Jareth.

"You are finished, Solistima" he said in a low hiss.

He gripped the sun pendant with his hand and ripped it from Jareth's chest, leaving a large wound where it had bound to his chest. Jareth let out a cry of pain like no one had ever heard before. His mother was standing across the courtyard and upon witnessing this, she began to sob uncontrollably and was reaching out for her son when Stromvir put himself in front of her.

He stood facing Lord Granok, he gripped his sword with all his might. He knew he would meet his demise should he make a move, he needed to wait for Granok to make the first move.

"Enough of this." Granok groaned as he stamped his staff on the marble ground, causing it to splinter in all directions. Stromvir's feet lifted off the ground. He was floating into the air, unable to control his body. He must have been about ten feet up when suddenly he was thrown down to the marble ground. He felt his shoulder break as he crashed into the ground. He tried to get up, but he seemed to be stuck to the ground.

Yojano stood up and turned to face Lord Granok. Before he could say anything, Granok tapped his staff on the ground to reveal his prisoners on their knees opposite them. They were bound by the hands and feet, on their knees and chained together. The look upon Yojano's face as he looked down at the five people Granok had bound together was that of sheer terror and hopelessness. Looking back up at him were the faces of his wife Tulan, son Theodore, Severus, Sarana, and Jareth's cousin Karavena.

CHAPTER 18

WHAT COMES NEXT

Yojano looked frantically between the faces of his loved ones before him. He had no idea what he could do for them. He had never seen or heard of anything like this before. He had no defenses against it, he had no known way of fighting back. He was at the mercy of Lord Granok now. Jareth, the one person he knew for certain could stop him, lay on the ground a few feet away clutching his chest in agonizing pain. Yojano knew he could not fight Granok, but perhaps there was another way.

Lord Granok turned and walked over to Jareth, who had managed to prop himself up against the marble wall behind him.

"I've had enough of you." Granok said as he pointed his staff at Jareth and then pointed it toward the sky. Within seconds, Jareth could feel himself being lifted into the air. He was powerless to stop it without his sun pendant. His body became limp and he struggled to keep his eyes open. He could feel himself moving faster and faster, he could feel himself being pulled in two separate directions, as if two forces were fighting over him. He heard a soft whisper in his head.

"Return, Solistima."

He could not see where he was, he could not even open his eyes. He was not sure if he was dead, but he was also not sure if he was alive. He knew there was something, he could feel it. Something warm and bright, something that seemed to uplift him, something that seemed to be the very essence of his life force. He heard the whisper again.

"Return…"

Jareth began to understand that he was being recalled to where he was given this power. He was floating toward the sun. He was getting closer, the warmth grew warmer, the light grew brighter. He heard the whisper for the final time.

"Rest, Solistima"

Lord Granok laughed as he saw Jareth being lifted through the air and out of sight. Jarena let out a deafening cry of despair as she watched.

"Once again, the Solistima is no more!" Granok yelled. "Does anybody else wish to step forward and face me?"

Seconds passed in silence. Granok raised his staff and pointed it toward the prisoners. Desperately, Yojano yelled with much plea in his voice.

"Stop! Let them go, it's me you really want." Yojano said as he raised both of his hands in surrender. "Let them go, and I will be your prisoner in their stead. I know this land and this castle better than any of them. My continued presence here would prove far more useful to you than theirs."

Yojano looked at the prisoners as he said this. He caught the eye of Severus, who had never looked so angry. Severus was shaking his head almost imperceptibly at Yojano. They stared at one another for a moment more before Yojano nodded and turned to his wife, who was holding the two-year-old Theodore in her arms. He gave her a look that told her everything she needed to know.

"There is truth in what you say, but why should I let five servants go to be left with one?" Granok asked, sneering.

"Five prisoners will prove more difficult to look after. You have five people to worry about escaping. Things could get out of hand and quickly" Yojano replied.

"You dare think I cannot handle my own prisoners?! I could take you all as my prisoners!" Granok bellowed.

"Yes, but again, with more numbers comes more risks. Surely you do not want an uprising on your hands" Yojano said calmly.

Granok seemed to think about this question for a while. It was true, an uprising was the last thing he needed. He of course knew that he could handle it should such an uprising occur.

"Mighty brave aren't we Yojano?" Granok asked as he approached him slowly.

"I am simply doing what must be done." Yojano said.

"I believe, we have an agreement." Granok replied. At that moment, the prisoners seemed to break free from the invisible bindings and were able to stand. They all rushed toward Yojano in an attempt to thank him, but they were knocked back before they could reach him.

"I said I would release them, but I never said you could speak to them. After all, a talk with them could lead to an uprising, or no?" Granok said with a smug look on his face. He began to laugh once more. He called for some of his men to come to where the prisoners stood.

"Lord Granok has showed you mercy this day. Should our paths ever cross in these circumstances again, I will have no mercy to show." He said. "You will be citizens of the New Gremela, I advise you all to fall in line like everyone else." He said to the prisoners as he made a hand gesture to his men. The men all began to lead the prisoners from the courtyard and across the bridge. Yojano tried to catch each one's attention before they vanished from sight.

Lord Granok's men continued on, each with their own prisoner in tow. When they were beyond the city gates they all went in separate directions, taking each prisoner to a different end of the empire. It would be almost impossible for them to find each other after this.

There would be no communication. Granok would surely shut down pixie usage for citizens.

Severus and Serana had not been separated, and neither had Tulan and Theodore. It was Karavena who was the only one that was alone. Lucky for her she had been led to the western coast of Gremela, where she and Jareth previously resided in Drahmstar.

Severus and Serana were simply dumbfounded at what happened. They were not sure why Yojana had done what he did, or why. Perhaps he knew something they didn't, perhaps he had a plan.

Tulan and Theodore were led east, somewhere they had never been before. She clutched her son in her hands and refused to let go. They had to stick together, she knew Yojano would come and find them eventually, she trusted him. The man she knew could make his way out of any situation. It was only a matter of time before she would see him again, but how much time?

Argosh and Octavia retreated to the beach where they met Stromvir, Jarena and Tullamore, they all began to discuss what would come next. Argosh and Octavia informed them they needed to return to Centauria, but they would return as soon as they could. They had to ensure Centauria did not meet the same fate. They told them they would send word to them in a few weeks' time. Argosh place his hand on Octavia's back and with a loud crack, they were gone again.

Yojano was standing on the terrace of the castle on the sea, watching as his loved ones were led away to an unknown fate. He knew this was for the best, and he knew placing himself at the side of Lord Granok would prove wise for everyone. He could study him, learn his habits, learn his weaknesses, his strengths, learn what drove him mad. Yojano had no idea how long it would be until he would see his friends again, but he knew it would be soon enough.

"How noble you are, Yojano. Staying on as my servant to free your friends." Granok said pompously. Yojano ignored Granok, instead he looked at him with those penetrating eyes that were still a dark shade of scarlet.

Granok raised his staff and Yojano's hands were tied behind his back, his legs shackled together, and his ornate robes turned to burlap rags and his feet became bare. He was no doubt being led to his quarters, his new home. Surely he would make use of the small jail cell in the dungeons of the castle. This was the cell that Tullamore occupied for some time. The thought of being on the other side made Yojano shutter. Granok shoved Yojano into the cell roughly and watched as he tumbled to the floor. He waited until Yojano had turned around to face him before slamming the bars shut and laughing as he walked away.

Meanwhile, just beyond the gates of the city, Tullamore, Stromvir and Jarena were planning. They knew they would need to stick together to have any chance at rescuing Yojano and defeating Granok. Tullamore knew of a safehouse nearby where they could stay. This place was tucked away in a small forest and took great knowledge of the area to be able to find. Tullamore and the members of his militia had used this place as a hideout before.

The three of them were on their way to the safehouse when they suddenly heard a deafening bang, followed by a flash. They looked up and saw the sun was emitting a blinding light. The sky turned a brilliant mixture of red and orange. Moments later, the three of them heard a beautiful noise filling the air. Stromvir knew what it was. He looked to the skies to see the beautiful phoenix he had seen so often before. It circled above the three of them for some time before finally descending and landing gracefully on a low hanging branch of a nearby tree. The three of them ran towards it, and much to their surprise it let them get within arm's reach. It sat on the tree looking at the three of them with wonder. Stromvir gazed into the blue marble-like eyes of the phoenix and seemed to get lost in them. The blue eyes pierced him like an arrow straight from the string of a bow, and he suddenly was filled with an unending sense of hope. He could feel the hope swelling up inside him, filling his body to the very brim. The others seemed to be experiencing a similar sensation, the grim looks upon their faces suddenly switched to a face of hopefulness and joy, a sense of wonder, a sense, that perhaps everything would be okay in the end.

Stromvir, still being within arm's reach of the bird, reached his hand out to embrace the phoenix. The great bird bowed its head to accept Stromvir's gentle pat, nuzzling its red and gold crest feathers on Stromvir's shoulder in return. The pain in Stromvir's shoulder went away and he realized what the bird had done. Just then, the bird took off with a powerful flap of its great wings and flew across the skies singing its song for all of Gremela to hear, instilling hope across the once peaceful land.

Jareth

Stromvir

Jarena

Yojano (22)

Yojano (49)

Severus

Sarana

Octavia

Resnik

Argosh

Made in United States
Orlando, FL
11 May 2024